Jordan,

I hope you enjoy
reading and, if you
I hope these will hel[p]
begin to love reading.

Roche[lle]
10/13/19

M000206041

Robert Starnes

An Exciting and Adventurous way to view History

Book One of the

Saving History Series

Time

Keeper

Robert Starnes

Robert Starnes

Published by Starnes Books LLC
Edited by Carpenter Editing Services, LLC

ISBN: 978-0-692-14959-1 (sc)
ISBN: 978-1-7325803-0-5 (e)

Printed in the United States of America
First Printing, 2018

Dedication

This book is dedicated to my nephew, Jaxson. It is through his strength and uniqueness which gave me the courage to be tested and ultimately diagnosed with ASD. So, because of him, I am able to be who I am meant to be completely and creatively. So "Thank You", Jax.

Robert Starnes

Contents

Robert Starnes

Contents

Prologue: Junior

Junior is sitting in his room trying to figure out how, and if, he is going to be able to stop the future from changing. He is not sure who or why, but someone has gone back and made changes in history. Those changes will soon catch up to his timeline and alter his future, forever.

Junior has been having visions of a future, in the form of blurred dreams, changing in some very bizarre ways. Some of these blurred visions include him while others do not. These visions are always in the form of one of two outcomes; either total mass destruction of all life on Earth, or the aftermath of a great war with only the survivors to rebuild Earth. Junior does not like either one of these two outcomes. He knows these may be future memories as well because of his own family's history. Yet he figures something is wrong, or soon will be, and he has to do something about the past before time runs out.

Junior does the only thing he thinks he can do which is to take out the gift given to him on his eighteenth birthday. The gift his mother gave him was from a family friend is was no longer with them in life. She told him stories about the gift being given down through her friend's family for generations. The family friend gave the gift to his mother, before he passed, in hopes that she would give it to Junior when he turned eighteen.

Junior grasps the gift, takes his place on his bed, lays back, opens his mind and begins to recall the stories his mother told him about her younger years. With any hope to save his future, Junior needs to go back and find his mother's childhood friend, Ian. He is unsure exactly how he is going to contact Ian, even if this works, but from the stories he was told about the Time Keeper it just may be possible.

So his search begins with him opening his mind and thinking back on the memories he was told of Ian. The rest is up to the Time Keeper and its powers.

I hope this works, Junior thinks to himself, as he fades into a deep state of unconsciousness...

Chapter 1

Birthday Surprise

Ian is a typical high school student except for the fact that he obtains higher than average grades and never misses a day of school. The only thing different about today is that it is his birthday. Today Ian is seventeen, and he is determined to make today an unrivaled day. Little did he know how perfect, this particular day, would turn out to be.

Ian may be a regular high school student, but he manages to avoid any drama that relates to high school. He avoids things like gossip, drugs, sex and bullying. Ian attends a public high school in Brooklyn that is filled with over aggressive, muscular guys his age with less than average IQs. Ian is not a muscular guy, yet despite this he is still able to be himself at school. Ian may not hold knowledge of what the future holds for him, but his feelings towards his classmates is that high school would be the peak of their lives. Ian is not going to let high school be the peak of his life. No way!

Ian woke up earlier this morning to the usual "Happy Birthday" from his parents, the phone calls from his grandparents, and a text message from his best friend Kayla. For Ian, today is just another day, just another birthday. For Ian's mother, today being Ian's birthday is special. She makes him his favorite breakfast of eggs over medium, butter toasted bread, and a short stack of buttermilk pancakes. *She appears happy today, more than her usual happy self. What is so different about today besides it being my birthday?* Ian wonders as he devours his scrumptious birthday breakfast.

After breakfast came the time to open his birthday present. Ian is aware of the difficult financial year his parents are experiencing since his father's recent layoff from work. His father worked for the *New York Times* for many years and had expected a larger severance package than he received. The small amount he received was in thanks due to the failed negotiations between the CEO of the *Times* and their Union President. Those negotiations cut the severance packages in half. This left Ian's parents with his mother's meager substitute teacher salary and the small severance from the *Times* as their only sources of income. Ian's parents did not let their financial hardship interfere in saving enough money to buy him one special gift this year for his seventeenth birthday.

Ian loves to stop by an antique bookstore after school every day. The bookstore, not one of the bookstore chains but a small family owned store that sells more than new books, is what makes this store a favorite of Ian's. This is a bookstore that sells first edition collections, antique jewelry, pins, and even notepads among other items. After two weeks of debating on what to buy Ian for his birthday this year, his parents decided on a unique timepiece sitting in the window of the bookstore that Ian had kept an eye on for some time now.

This particular antique bookstore is a getaway place for Ian. This bookstore is a place where he is able to be himself. He does not worry about what other kids think of his skinny build or of his intelligence. He experiences the emotions of not being a normal high school student at this bookstore. This enjoyment enables him the freedoms of the world. The freedom he gets is from being lost for hours on end in the stories he reads. Ian has always loved reading. At the age of four years old Ian taught himself how to read. That's when Ian's love of reading began and when his parents recognized him as a gifted child.

Ian's mother cleared off the table and took the dishes into the kitchen to wash. She soon returned with a small gift for Ian. The wrapping was in a very modest, shiny, silver paper, with a hand crafted white lace bow on top. Ian's intuition tells him the gift wrapping is by a professional. For many years he has seen his parents' wrappings, and this does not compare to any of their previous attempts.

"This is the nicest gift wrapping you ever attempted before."

"Thank you, but we paid for gift wrapping at the store." Even though money is tight, they spent the extra money on having this gift wrapped at the shop.

Ian, not wanting to appear like he doesn't care of the extra cost they paid for the wrapping, takes his time opening his gift. Ian can tell his parents want him to open the box quicker by the expressions on their faces. Ian takes their expressions of anticipation to heart and opens the box the way they intended for him to do. Ian opens the top of the box which begins to reveal the timepiece he's been eyeing at the bookstore.

"This is the most wonderful gift I ever received before, but it's way too expensive," Ian tells his parents. "With all you have been through money wise this year, I know this is out of your budget. I appreciate the gesture, but you have more important things the money should be used for besides a birthday gift for me."

"Ian, we've been preparing for this day for a very long time, and this timepiece is going to help guide you," his father speaks up. "Now go make yourself presentable for the day, because we've got another surprise for you."

Unsure what his father means by, 'help guide you,' Ian gives his parents a hug for the amazing gift and goes to his bedroom to dress for the day.

Autumn is beginning, so Ian decides on a pair of faded jeans, a purple button down shirt, black vest, belt, shoes, and a light jacket to shield him from the brisk New York autumn breeze. Ian, who's always been a snappy dresser, is ready for the day. Or at least he thinks he's ready.

Ian reaches for his bedroom door knob, then turns around to grab the timepiece his parents had given him for his birthday, except the watch appears to be missing. At least Ian thinks the watch is missing. He glances at his wrist and sees the watch wrapped around it! *Did I put the watch on and forget?* Ian wonders.

With no more thoughts about how the watch ended up on his wrist, Ian opens his bedroom door and starts his way down the hall past the kitchen and into the living room. Ian is expecting to find his parents waiting for him with the other birthday surprise his father had mentioned earlier, but the surprise is that he is alone. His parents are nowhere to be found.

"Hello, mom, dad, are you here?" No reply.

Ian's parents do not usually leave without telling him first. His parents always leave him a note if they plan on going out somewhere.

Ian looks on the kitchen counter, on the dining room table, and on the coffee table, but finds no note from either of his parents. He did not find any explanation of where they may have gone.

Where are they? They must have gone to get the other part of the surprise for me, Ian thinks.

After waiting ten minutes, Ian decides to go search for his parents. Unsure where to begin, he remembers that his mother loves Central Park. Then a thought shoots into his mind like a photograph. He recognizes Belvedere Castle. He always enjoys going on tours of the castle, because he loves the history of the castle. The castle was built in 1869 as a Victorian folly, which at the time was considered an expensive ornamental building with a mock Gothic tower. Since the castle was built on the second highest natural elevation of the park, the views across Central Park and New York City were quoted as second to none. The news of the castle closing to the public in the 1960's was no secret, and later it was renovated and reopened again to the public in 1983. Ian fell in love with Belvedere Castle even more when he found out it was home to Count von Count from Sesame Street, which was one of his favorite childhood TV shows.

Ian leaves their small, two bedroom apartment, locks the door, and heads down the hall to the stairwell. They have lived in this third floor walkup his entire life, and the elevator's been broken for as long as he can remember. Oh well, the exercise does him good.

As Ian came to the bottom of the stairs, the cool autumn air breezed through him.

I should have picked a heavier coat to wear today, because the wind is cold out here. Ian's mission to find his parents is his top priority, so he decides to keep the light jacket he chose and continue on his way. Ian has no time to waste in finding his parents.

Ian exits the apartment building. Knowing the distance is too far to ride his bike, he hails a taxi to take him to Central Park. Ian is lucky enough to flag down the first taxi that passes by his building.

Ian opens the taxi door and takes a seat as the driver turns and asks, "Where to?"

"West 81st Street and Central Park West." The address is no mystery to Ian as many times as he has been to Belvedere Castle, even after his mother stopped taking him once he got older.

Ian does not like to take taxis anywhere. He hates the horrible odor. It's as if all the previous passengers' body odors and cheap perfumes during the past year are still lingering. Ian not only dislikes the foul odors, he also hates the way taxi drivers' drive. Taxi drivers seem to drive with their eyes closed. They honk their horns, yell at people walking by, and switch lanes without looking first. This scares Ian more than anything in the world. He cannot wait to end this heart stopping ride.

As they make their way into the city from Brooklyn taking the Manhattan Bridge, Ian senses something change while crossing over the bridge. Not only did Ian sense something different within himself, but his arm vibrates a little. On reflex, when his arm begins to vibrate, Ian glances down at his arm to check out what could be causing the vibration. That is when he passes out cold in the backseat of the taxi.

Chapter 2

Ian's Year

Ian leaves for school and attends his first semester.

Ian comes home for winter break.

Ian goes back to school.

Ian continues with his second semester.

Ian does have a summer break at school.

Ian finishes his senior year.

Now Ian gets to go home in time for his birthday.

Chapter 3

School Without Ian

Now that Ian is going to a new school without her, Kayla is not sure how she will survive their senior year without him. They both have attended the same schools together their entire lives, so this is going to be quite a change for her. Even though being away from Ian will be hard for her, she understands how hard things will be for Ian as well. *Ian will be at his school for a year, but he will be home for the holidays,* Kayla thinks to herself. She finishes getting ready for her first day school as a senior.

Kayla is ready for school, so she gathers up her school bag, yells 'Goodbye' to her mother and heads out of the front door. Kayla makes her way down the hallway and into the stairwell when she thinks she hears someone say her name. For a moment her first thought is of Ian, but then she remembers he is going to another school this year. Logically thinking she may have left something behind at home, it maybe her mother calling her back, so she stops in the hall. Kayla looks back at her apartment door, but when she glances back to check, it's closed. Then her name is spoke again but this time louder and coming from the stairwell. Kayla whips her head around and makes her way to the doorway of the stairwell to see who is calling her name.

Kayla enters through the doorway and meets a woman she does not know. She is unsure if this is who has been calling her name. Kayla not wanting to be rude, excuses herself as she tries to pass, but the mysterious woman stands and does not move. She stands in the same spot with the same expression on her face. Kayla is not sure how to take the woman's expression. She interprets it as either surprise or fear, but either way it begins to makes her uncomfortable. She is about to turn and go back to her apartment to grab her mother, but the woman stops her with one question, "Kayla?"

Something about the way the woman speaks her name makes Kayla stop. She can feel that the woman is not going to hurt her.

"Kayla? Your name is Kayla, correct?" the woman questions.

"I have a sense you are aware of who I am as you have said my name, twice to be exact, before you are now asking me my name. How are we acquainted with each other, because something is giving me a notion we are," Kayla demands from the woman.

"Well, we first met a long time ago. I can't believe you remember so far back. You were so young," the woman tells Kayla.

"Well, I wouldn't say I remember meeting you, but there is something in the way you speak my name that seems familiar. The tone in your voice makes me suspect we've met before. I hate to sound rude, but who are you?" Kayla ponders to the strange woman in the stairwell.

"Oh, I'm so sorry. My name is Alexis. I don't mean to keep you from school if that's where you are going. I'm sorry, but when you said "goodbye" to your mother, I was not sure if I was hearing your voice or not. I, being unsure, said your name the first time. The sound of your voice startled me. I am on my way up to visit Ian, and I have a birthday gift for him," Alexis finishes.

"Oh, so you are also acquainted with Ian? Well, you are a little late. Ian's birthday was last week, and he left for a private school for our senior year a few days ago," Kayla fills Alexis in.

"Time is not on my side these days," Alexis whispers in a pleasant but sad sounding way. "Do you know what school Ian is attending?"

"No, but the school is not here in the city. I assume that is why they left a few days ago," smirks Kayla.

"Oh, is someone else going with Ian to this private school?"

"Not that I am aware. Why do you ask?" Kayla retorts back.

"Well, you said 'they left a few days ago', when I asked about Ian going to school. So I assume someone else is going with him," wonders Alexis.

"Oh yes, he's one of Ian's new teachers. I don't recall his name, but he came from the school to pick Ian up and take him back. I think he is a friend of Ian's parents," Kayla clears her comments up.

"Oh yes, you're right," Alexis speaks with a soft tone to herself.

"Did you say something?" Kayla inquires.

"Well, now I need to come up with a way to be able to give this gift to Ian. I can't come back next year, and he will need this gift," Alexis conveys with a little desperation in her voice.

"Well, I need to be on my way to school. I don't want to be late on my first day as a senior. Sorry you missed Ian. The next time I hear from him I will relay the message you are looking for him and about the gift you have for him as well. I'm not sure when it will be, but I will make sure he gets the message," Kayla assures Alexis. After she assures Alexis, she makes her way around her to the other side of the stairs leading down to the street.

"Thank you. Sorry to have kept you so long, and may I say how good bumping into you today's been. I hope we run into each other again soon. Now run along, if you don't leave at this moment you will miss your first bus connection to school," Alexis insists to Kayla.

Kayla gives Alexis a look of confusion and concern while running down the stairs, until she reaches the door which exits to the street. Just as she steps out of the exit doors of her apartment building, her first bus is about to shut their doors and leave. Kayla runs up to the closing doors in time to grab the driver's attention to open them back up so she can hop on, which almost made her miss her first connecting bus to school. Kayla strolls down the aisle looking for an empty seat to claim. Once she finds an empty seat and sits down, she cannot help but wonder if Alexis memorized the bus schedule, if she is good at guessing, or if she actually knew she was about to miss her bus. This is not what Kayla planned to be thinking about on the first day of school, but things change.

***

The sound of the final school bell of the day begins to set in with Kayla. She can't believe everything that's been happening to her today. *Did this all happen to me today? Did I endure the entire day?* Kayla is questioning herself. *Did I succeed through my first day of high school as a senior without Ian?*

Kayla's been anticipating this moment since her arrival at school this morning, so when the last bell sounds she is ready to head home. With so much excitement in her about her first day as a senior now over and being prepared for this moment, she had the things she needs to take home with her. With the bell ending her first day as a senior, she takes off out of her final class of the day and heads straight for the school exit. She is so full of energy she cannot decide if she wants to run, walk, or take a bus home from school. With this much energy, she decides she will take a walk, at least part of the way, and go from there as she grows closer to home. The only thing missing from the day being perfect for Kayla is not being able to share this moment with Ian. But she imagines he is going through the exact same thing she is which gives her a bit of comfort.

Kayla walks along the busy streets of Brooklyn not paying any attention to the daily foot traffic when she bumps into someone. The stranger turns and smiles at her as they both recognize each other. "Excuse me Alexis, I was not paying attention while I was walking. Are you okay?"

"I am fine. Thanks for asking. I am also sorry for bumping into you as well. I should have been paying more attention to my surroundings, but I was just sorting through my thoughts. So how was your first day of school as a senior?" Alexis acknowledges Kayla.

"Today was awesome! My senior year is going to be my easiest year yet. This is why I am walking home. I am too full of energy to sit on a bus all the way home. So, did you figure out what you are going to do about getting the gift you got for Ian to him?" Kayla takes interest in knowing.

"I was walking around today and I thought of a few options. This is why I am out here walking around. I like to walk around when I need to clear my head or make a decision. The noise of the city streets seems to reduce the thoughts inside my head and help me find the best choice in my mind," Alexis reveals.

"I do the exact same thing sometimes, so I can relate," Kayla shouts with excitement.

"Would you like some company walking home, or would you rather be alone to burn off all your energy?" Alexis hopes for a 'yes' from Kayla.

"Sure, I could use some company, and it sounds possible that we've got a lot in common," Kayla answers.

"Thank you for allowing me to walk with you. You are correct, I believe we may be more alike than you may think," Alexis smiles at Kayla.

The two of them take off down the street heading towards Kayla's apartment building. The walk is going to take them around forty-five minutes until they reach their destination, so during the walk they decide to find out a little more about each other. They make small talk about Kayla and Ian's friendship, growing up together, and how this is the first time they have ever been apart from each other. Kayla could talk to Alexis about Ian all day. Since Alexis came to visit Ian in the first place, Kayla felt Alexis wouldn't mind listening.

They talk the entire walk home. Suddenly, Kayla realizes they are standing outside her apartment building. She glances at Alexis and the two of them start laughing.

"I can't believe we are at my building already. The walk did not take long."

"You never can predict how fast time can run away from you when you are not focusing on time but focusing more on the people right in front of you at the moment. Do you recall ever being told the phrase, 'Time flies when you're having fun'? Well that's what it means," Alexis explains to Kayla.

"Thank you for walking home with me and allowing me to become reacquainted with you, but also it was like getting to meet you for the first time. It has been a pleasure, so if there is anything I can do to help you, please allow me the opportunity," Kayla mentions as she is saying her goodbye to Alexis.

"It has been very nice being reintroduced to you as well, but I am leaving today. Like I mentioned before, I will be unable to come back.

How would you take it if I gave you the gift I got for Ian and asked you to give the gift to him for his birthday next year?" Alexis prays Kayla will agree to accept the offer.

"I know asking this of you sounds strange, but all the other options I could think of don't seem to be workable. I mean after hearing how long you and Ian have been a part of each other's' lives and are as close as you are, I will trust my gift for him with you," Alexis pleads with Kayla.

"Well, giving Ian the gift you have for him sounds like something I can do for you. Would you like me to tell Ian anything about the gift, or you, when I give him the gift from you?" Kayla probes Alexis for more information.

"Why don't you just tell him you got him the gift and don't mention me? I didn't want to burden you with my health issues, but I will not be alive by the time Ian turns eighteen. You are not aware of this, but I am very sick, and I do not want Ian spending time looking for me when he should be out enjoying his own life. Thank you for telling me so much about Ian on the walk home from school today, and it sounds like the two of you experienced some great times together. Thank you for giving this to him as well," Alexis finishes as she hands over a small gift. The gift is wrapped in a smooth, elegant, black style wrapping paper with a white ribbon, which makes into a small bow on top.

Once Kayla accepts the gift and promises to give the gift to Ian on his eighteenth birthday for her, Alexis turns around and begins to walk away from Kayla but then she stops. Alexis turns back to Kayla and reaches out her hand. "Kayla, please accept this necklace as a thank you from me for everything you have done today and for passing on my gift to Ian." Alexis hands Kayla an antique necklace. The necklace is old with a small watch on its end.

Kayla opens her hand to receive the gift from Alexis as she turns her gaze down to view the gift being put in her possession. As Kayla looks up to face Alexis, she had already vanished into the crowd passing nearby. Kayla senses a bit of sadness rush over her. Even though she just met Alexis, she has sympathy for her on so many levels. Alexis came here to visit Ian one last time and to give him a gift before she dies. But her being unable to achieve either breaks Kayla's heart.

Kayla wipes a tear from her cheek as she turns around to make her way to the stairwell door to her apartment building. The energy she once had earlier was now gone. Kayla is very tired now, but she wants to go home and tell her mom how her first day as a senior went. She decides not to tell her mother about Alexis and wants their meeting to be something she keeps to herself as Alexis had wanted. Kayla walks up the stairs until she reaches her floor, walks through the doorway and down the hall to her apartment door. Kayla needs to take a moment before going inside to take a deep breath and relax herself. She puts a smile on her face and bursts into the apartment with excitement.

"Mom, I'm home! You will not believe the day I had today at school. This is going to be my easiest year ever," Kayla announces as she enters.

"Well, let me make us some tea so you can tell me all about your first day as a senior," her mother reassures her. Kayla's mother heads to the kitchen to makes their tea while Kayla takes a seat on the couch. Kayla waits for her mom to rejoin her so they can do their usual mother-daughter bonding they do every year after her first day of school.

Chapter 4

Ian's 18th Birthday Party

Kayla cannot believe Ian was on his way home from school. Ian and Kayla have been missing each other since winter break during the holidays. She's been missing him and is ready to give him the biggest hug she's ever given him before. Ian, during winter break, expressed how sad he was for being unable to attend her graduation due to his school's schedule and the way the school year ran through to the end of summer. Kayla wanted to cry after hearing the news, but she didn't. She could tell by his tone and the expression on his face, that he was hurting as much as she was. *That was then and this is now, and now he is on his way home.* Kayla, remembering that unpleasant night, decides to think of happier thoughts.

Ian's mother, along with Kayla helping her, set up their apartment for a surprise birthday party for Ian. She wants everything all set up and ready for the surprise for as soon as Ian walks in the door. The two of them decorate all morning and call some of his friends. His mother makes sure she has his favorite red velvet cake for his 'Special Day' as she keeps referring to today for some reason. Kayla begins to wonder why Ian's mother keeps repeating the same words again and again, "This is such a 'Special Day' for Ian." Kayla's been to every birthday party of Ian's, and his mother has never called any of them a 'Special Day.' Kayla thinks of the day the same way, because today is Ian's eighteenth birthday. But she does not understand why his mother needs to keep repeating the sentence so much, sometimes repeating it just to herself. Kayla just goes along with her, every time the words 'Special Day' come out of her mouth, and continues to do what's asked of her. She also wants today to be perfect for Ian's return.

The two of them continue setting up the decorations and making sure everything is right where it's supposed to be for the party. Once everything is in the exact place where Ian's mother planned it to be, they wait. Ian's mom invites a few of his friends over, or kids from school she thinks are his friends, and a few other guests who are unknown to Kayla. She figures they must either be relatives of theirs or friends of his parents. Finding out who they are is harder for her than she anticipates, since they are not the social type of people. They stand around speaking among themselves. Some of their neighbors from the building are at Ian's surprise party. *At least I am familiar with some of these people,* Kayla giggles to herself. *Let's take a glance around the room; there is 2C and 4D. Wait, is that 'Crazy Cat Lady' who lives on the top floor I spot sitting by the window?* Kayla begins checking out their neighbors who are in attendance. Kayla grows bored quicker than she thought with the neighbor calling game and decides to find out what time Ian should be arriving.

"What time is Ian supposed to arrive?" Kayla inquires of Ian's mother.

"Well, he should be here by now, but traffic is so unpredictable. I'm sure he will be here any minute now," his mother responds with no conviction in her own answer.

By the time she finishes, one more guest comes rushing into the apartment announcing that Ian has just pulled up in a taxi and for everyone to hide.

***

Ian is waking up in the backseat of the taxi. Not remembering falling asleep, he realizes something is different.

"Why is the sky so dark now?" Ian wonders to the cabbie, not noticing he is not the same driver which had picked him up from his apartment earlier.

The cabbie replies back with a simple, "Well, because the time is 9:30 P.M."

"How's it even possible for it to be so late? I hailed your cab a few minutes ago, at 9:15 A.M.," Ian explains. "How long have we been driving?" At this moment Ian can tell the cab driver is not the same one from this morning.

"We've been driving for about fifteen minutes. You did just hail my cab, but the time was about 9:15 P.M.," the cabbie replies.

What is going on? Ian questions himself. *How can this be?* But before Ian can even think of any possible answers to his own questions, he realizes something else. They are not driving towards the city any longer but away from the city.

"Excuse me, but may I ask where I hailed you from?" Ian needs clarification before more confusion can set in.

"You hailed my cab, and I picked you up at East 85th Street and Fifth Avenue. You were coming out of the building on the corner," the cabbie tells Ian. "Are you alright?"

"Yes, I'm fine, but humor me for a second. Where did I ask you to take me?"

"You asked me to take you to Brooklyn. You said to take you home. Do you need to go somewhere else instead?" the cabbie inquires with a bit of concern in his tone.

"No. Home is fine," whispers Ian. "Home is fine."

Ian decides to sit back and ride the rest of the way home in silence. As confused as he is, neither the aroma of the back of the cab nor the way this cabbie is driving, bother him today. Ian is lost in his own thoughts.

Ian wonders what is happening and why. *Where did the time go and where are my parents? Is this real, or can I be dreaming?* The only thing Ian can tell for a fact that is real is the fear inside of him.

Ian couldn't wait to arrive home. He has a sense of home is where he should be. He hopes his parents will be home when he arrives so he can ask them where they went this morning.

Anxiety is building up in Ian as the taxi pulls up to his apartment building. Ian pays the cabbie, jumps out of the cab and runs upstairs to the 3rd floor as fast as he can. Once he makes his way up the stairs, he sprints down the hallway to his front door. But he freezes in place, only for a split moment, when he realizes he is not wearing the same clothes he put on this morning.

Ian, letting the fact he is wearing different clothes, the sun is gone and the moon is out now, glimpses the apartment door and is surprised with the door being cracked open. That is when panic shoots through Ian's mind.

The party guests take cover in their hiding places, and Kayla can tell the front door is still ajar. She knows shutting the door will be too risky, since Ian is standing outside the door.

What is he waiting on? Kayla thinks, trying to avoid the cramp starting to ache in her leg from hiding.

With no more hesitation, Ian charges the door. Once inside, the lights come on and people are jumping out from everywhere. They are coming out from behind the couch, the hallway, the bedrooms, and from in the kitchen. Ian does not understand what is happening, until everyone is shouting, "Surprise, Happy Birthday Ian!"

Once Ian's heart slows down and the initial shock of panic leaves his frozen body, his mom enters the room holding a birthday cake. She is taking the cake into the kitchen. Ian thinks, *Could that be where they went, to buy my birthday cake?* Just at that moment Ian realizes he forgot today is his birthday.

Relief rushes over Ian because his parents are home and they are safe. He cannot help but let his mind wonder. *Where had they gone and what happened today in the taxi on the way to the park? Where did the time go?* He put those questions out of his mind for now.

Ian smiles at everyone who is at his party and thanks them for coming and surprising him on his birthday. He thinks, *if they had any clue this surprise almost killed me, and if they knew what I went through today, which is still a mystery even to me, they may have held back on the yelling part of my surprise.* Ian is thankful things are back to normal.

Kayla thinks, by the shock on his face, this surprise almost scared Ian to death. She follows him as his mom leads him to the head of the dining room table, while he is still thanking everyone for coming. Kayla cannot let go of the expression of shock on his face when he came in the door. She senses something is wrong with Ian, until he takes his seat and sees a gift. The gift sitting on the table is a small wrapped gift in black paper with a white ribbon tied in a bow on top with a card attached. He can tell the gift is from Kayla just by the handwriting of his name on the card. He glances up and locks eyes with his best friend Kayla. That is the moment when the expression of worry on his face changes to relief. This, in turn, makes Kayla begin to fret, because she is going to tell Ian about the gift from Alexis, except she will be telling a lie. A lie she's been practicing for a year without even knowing what the gift is. She's beginning to panic. She's doubting the story she's created over the past year, and Ian is going to see right through her. Kayla sighs with relief as Ian's mom brings out his cake. This means the gifts and her lie can wait for now.

Ian is only able to relax after being able to make eye contact with his best friend Kayla. The two of them grew up together, and they both live in the same apartment building and attend the same schools. Ian cannot wait to tell her about the events of his day. She may be able to help him fill in some of his missing time. Ian is unable to call

Kayla over to the table to bring up the events of his day before his mother sets his birthday cake down in front of him. It reads, "Happy 18th Birthday Ian!"

"What is this?"

"It's your birthday cake. I got your favorite, red velvet."

"Why is 'Happy 18th Birthday' on it?"

"Well, because you are eighteen today silly," she replies. His mother gives him a hint of worry, then asks, "How are you feeling?"

Ian is filled with the possibility of hitting his head in the cab on his way to Central Park and then forgetting about what happened while he was in the park. Ian knows that there is no way he hit his head hard enough to forget an entire year of this life. Ian cannot hold back his concerns any longer. Now he really is worried.

Not knowing how to answer his mother's question, overwhelmed with fear and confusion with what's been happening today, he only nods his head.

"Something's not right here," Ian states. "Is this some kind of joke? If it is a joke, I can tell you this is not a funny one." Ian is ready to rise up from the table and run out of the apartment, and then he realizes he cannot move. He is frozen stiff with fear.

What is going on here? What is he talking about? Kayla is asking herself. Now she's worrying about Ian and is certain the expression on his face is a sign of something to do with it.

"You did not answer your mom's question. How are you? You have a strange expression on your face," Kayla is speaking.

Kayla compares Ian's strange expression with a story from their past. "That's one expression you have shown only once before, and it was the time we decided to watch a horror movie after your parents had gone to bed. Man, that movie scared us so bad, neither of us could sleep without the lights on for two weeks." This brought out a few laughs from the guests, but not from Ian.

After Kayla finishes her story, Ian's father speaks.

"I think you may need to go lie down and rest son. You don't appear well."

"Yes, Ian, listen to your father. If you wake up tomorrow and you are not any better, we will go visit Dr. Allen," Ian's mother insists. "How does that sound?"

Ian takes a quick scan around the room and then excuses himself from his party to go to his room and rest. "Yes, some rest is what I need. Today's been a long day. I will talk to you tomorrow," speaking directly to Kayla. "Thank you all again for coming tonight, and I apologize for excusing myself early. I am thankful you all came tonight.

Also, Mother, Father, thank you as well for throwing such an amazing surprise party for my birthday. I'm blessed having you for parents."

With that, Ian turns and leaves his surprise birthday party.

Ian retreats to go to his room to rest. Kayla asks Ian's mother if she wants any help cleaning up or anything, but his mom assures her she can handle it. She thanks Kayla and says she should go home and come back in the morning to check on Ian. Kayla thanks her, says her goodbye, promises to return in the morning and heads out the door.

Ian walks down the hall to his bedroom door, opens it, walks in and closes it behind him. Ian's room appears to be the same as it did when he left this morning, which is comforting to him.

Kayla walks down the hallway to the stairs that lead down to her floor, only one flight down, and she cannot help but wonder what is going on with Ian. She could tell something was wrong with him from the moment he walked in the front door. It did not register with anyone else at the party, until Ian started freaking out about it being his eighteenth birthday. Kayla, being his best friend, was aware something was not right.

Kayla makes it down to her floor and down the hall to her door, grabs the knob and lets herself in. She is calling it a night. After the long day with Ian's mom decorating and setting up for Ian's party, she needs some rest of her own and she wants to check on Ian first thing in the morning.

Now, Ian's back in his room and everyone's left the party, he is so exhausted from everything that has happened during the day, all Ian wants to do is rest. Ian sits down on his bed to remove his shoes, falls over, and before long he is fast asleep.

Chapter 5

What Truths Dreams Hold

Ian wakes up startled by not being in his own bedroom where he had fallen asleep last night. The room he wakes up in has gray concrete walls covered in oversized paintings. *Where am I?* Ian wonders. *This is not my room!*

Ian picks himself up and out of the enormous, four post bed he found himself in and realizes he is still wearing the same clothes he fell asleep in at home. He hurries over to the window at the other end of the room. As he glances out of the window, he is taken aback by seeing a field outlining a beautiful forest. "This is not Brooklyn," Ian exhales!

Ian, now verifying he is no longer in his own room or in Brooklyn for that matter, takes a detailed view of his surroundings. After a closer inspection of the elegant four post bed, he looks up to find arches of the cathedral ceilings above him. The room does not have many furnishings except for two hand crafted, wood, wingback chairs, which sit atop a most exquisite handmade rug.

The huge wood frame paintings which hang on the majority of the walls must be members of the family for many generations past and each have been painted with the utmost of care. The cathedral ceilings are painted with angels and biblical themes with amazing stroke work and care.

The same handmade rugs cover only the parts where the wood flooring and the furniture come in contact with each other. Otherwise the wood floor is bare to show off its natural beauty throughout the room.

In this room, one wall is covered with bright red wallpaper. The wallpaper is also covered with a symbol which may be a family crest. The bright red wallpaper, in contrast with the eggshell white paint of the trim of the wood burning fireplace, stands out to Ian. White paint covers the complete exterior, including the mantel, with gold paint trim accenting the center of the opening and bottom of the six foot tall fireplace. No fire was burning inside of the fireplace, although one may have been before from the looks of it. The room's ceiling is beautiful and has a crystal candle chandelier hanging from it which is lit and putting out enough light for Ian to enjoy his luxurious view.

Ian is beginning to enjoy the breathtaking views from the room, when without warning, the room changes. He is no longer in a bedroom fit for a king but now he is in a room fit for children.

Ian now sits in a classroom that does not resemble any classroom he's been in before since everything appears aged. The desks are designed to seat two students each and are made of a hardwood, which is as uncomfortable to sit in as it appears to be. After a few minutes of sitting at the desk, he starts moving around. He cannot imagine having to sit at one of these desks for an entire day of school.

The room is empty of people, students or a teacher; however, there is a desk at the head of the room. The desk sits in front of an old chalkboard with the alphabet stenciled across the top. Ian assumes this to be the teacher's desk. Between the chalkboard and the teacher's desk is a single wood chair that he assumes is just a little less uncomfortable as the other desks for the students. The top of the teacher's desk has a bright red apple sitting all alone. *That apple must be from the teacher's pet,* Ian thinks to himself for amusement.

Ian continues to take in his surroundings of the old classroom, taking in the old styles that differ from the modern day classrooms like the ones at his school. One thing that sticks out in his mind is the lack of overhead lighting. Ian spots some shelving that hangs on the wall behind the teacher's desk. On the shelving sit two oil lamps, which must be used to illuminate the classroom when needed. "I guess staying late for extra credit is out of the question," Ian mocks aloud to himself, since he would be the type of student to stay for extra credit.

Ian walks across the old hardwood floor of the classroom towards a freestanding wooden globe. As he does so, the floor beneath his feet creeks. Ian redirects his focus down and can tell the floors need to be polished or waxed. It's like the floors were installed and used with little, to no, upkeep afterwards. Ian is returning his attention back to the antiquated globe, when he finds something even better, a wood burning furnace. This wood burning furnace is small with a metal pipe that comes out of the top and goes straight through the top of the ceiling and out of the building. "Guess this is used to keep the smoke from filling the room. What were they thinking?" Ian's shaking his head in disbelief of what he is seeing.

"How could they put a wood burning furnace sitting on an old wood floor next to old wooden school desks? How could they not worry about burning down a building full of children? A building built like this nowadays would never pass inspections, and parents would flip-out." The changes over time are extreme to Ian.

Ian starts to turn his attention to the opposite side of the classroom where an old, interesting looking piano is sitting. Then he hears the muffled sounds two boys arguing from outside. Ian is making his way over to the closest window which is next to one of the wooden student school desks, and he trips over the stand that is holding the oversized globe. His clumsiness sends the globe to the hardwood floor landing with a thud and rolling away. Ian thinks little about the noise the globe's landing made, since he is just dreaming, but the boys stop arguing. Ian's afraid the boys heard the noise inside the building.

"Is someone in the school? Who are you?" yells one of the boys from outside the building.

Ian is unable to peek outside the window, answer back, or even figure out what is going on before things change again and Ian is gone.

Ian is sitting on a park bench in Central Park. *Why does this keep happening to me?* Ian questions. This place is familiar to him. This bench in Central Park is out in front of Belvedere Castle.

Could I have been in Belvedere Castle before ending up here? How is this even possible? Ian wants some answers, and fast, before something else happens.

The more Ian thinks about the two rooms he was in, first the bedroom and then the classroom, the less he understands what is happening to him.

Now Ian begins to think that either yesterday was a dream, and he dozed off at the park, or this is a dream and he is at home asleep in his bed. To Ian, either one of these could be reality.

Ian is unsure how long he's been sitting on the park bench but just as he is about to hop up, without warning, a stranger sits down beside him. The strange man is dressed in a tracksuit, running shoes, and red headphones that hang around his neck. He appears to be someone taking a break from running in the park. Before Ian can turn and ask the man where they are, the man reaches over and grabs Ian by his wrist. Surprised by the forwardness and roughness of the stranger, Ian tries to pull his arm back, but the stranger's grip is too strong.

"Ian, don't be afraid. We met once before, but I am betting you don't remember, do you?" Came the voice of the mysterious man as if he can read the puzzled expression on Ian's face.

"That is possible. When did we meet?" Ian inquires; as he could be a possible friend of his parents. Ian has met several of his parents' friends on many occasions in the past, and he cannot remember them all. The last thing any teenager wants is to be friends with any of his parents' friends.

"Well, that is hard to say," replies the man in the track suit. "The answer will depend on which birthday you are having today. Is today your seventeenth or eighteenth birthday?"

Ian is unsure how this man could guess today is his birthday, much less the fact that Ian himself does not understand which of his birthdays he was having today. Ian takes a moment to gather his thoughts and then asks some of his own questions.

"For starters, how are you sure today is my birthday? Second, what does my age have to do with anything?" He thinks that he is not the only person having memory problems today. This is a relief to him. The inquisitive stranger concedes, after taking into consideration Ian's concerns. "Okay, those are two fair points you make. What I am about to tell you may sound crazy, but please let me finish," the man requests. "Is that a deal?"

"Fine," Ian agrees.

"I can assure you today's your birthday, because I met you on your seventeenth birthday. Your parents asked me to come meet you, as a favor to them and I agreed. But since we met, things have changed and became a little harder to explain," the stranger admits.

"You are starting to sound like a crazy person to me," Ian chimes in.

"Please Ian, let me finish and if enough time is left for questions I will answer them. Do you agree to this?" the strange man cuts Ian off and goes back to telling his story.

"My name is Jax, and I am a teacher at a school for bright students like yourself. Your parents gave you a birthday gift which has been in your family for many generations which holds unique powers. You don't understand how to access the powers yet, but you did access them one year ago today by accident, which is why today is your eighteenth birthday. We do not have much time left in this moment, but your dreams are actual moments in time that are stored in the Time Keeper. Try and remember what you can about each memory, and we will discuss them when our time to meet for the first time comes."

"I can't tell you everything at this moment, because time is going to change. I do need to tell you more, but not now. You will understand very soon," Jax promises.

Right after that, just like the times before, the dream changes and Ian is gone. He is no longer in the park. Ian now finds himself at a party.

This was not a normal party, but more of an event. *Who are all these old people?* Ian wonders to himself.

Ian hopes this is a dream, well, more of a nightmare than a dream. "The thought of old people having a party is a nightmare for sure!" Ian chuckles to himself.

From the appearance of this place, the room he is in is on the top floor penthouse of a high-rise in Manhattan. From the floor-to-ceiling windows, Ian can make out Belvedere Castle. The room is massive, wall to wall windows giving a panoramic view. Not only can Ian see Belvedere Castle in Central Park, but as he turns around he can see the entire city of New York City.

Ian knows he can flash away again at any moment now, so he turns his focus on to the people in the room. Ian turns his gaze from one person to the next, but does not seem to recognize anyone. Then all at once, he spots Jax, the man from the park. He is no longer wearing a tracksuit, but he is in a very exquisite tuxedo with a bright red bowtie. As Ian starts towards Jax to speak to him, he peeks down at his wrist to check the time, but the Time Keeper is gone!

He can confirm one thing for sure, that watch means more to him than any other gift he's ever received before because of what his parents gave up for him for his birthday. To him, the watch is irreplaceable. Ian looks back up and walks towards Jax, but before he can reach him, he is awakened by someone knocking on his bedroom door.

Chapter 6

Kayla's Gift

The next morning could not come quickly enough for Kayla, since she was worried about what happened to Ian last night at his party. All she could think about was the look on his face when he burst through the front door of his apartment last night. She knew something was wrong then and wants to make sure he is okay today.

"Mom, I'm going to run up and check on Ian. I will be back in a little while," Kayla shouts to her mother.

"Don't be gone too long. Remember we are supposed to go shopping today, just the two of us, a girl's day," her mother replies.

"Oh yeah, sorry, I forgot. Okay, I won't be long. He did not appear well when he came home last night, so we did not have time to talk," Kayla fills her mother in on a portion of the action of last night's reunion. "I'll be back in a few."

Kayla takes off out of the apartment and makes her way up to Ian's as fast as she can. Upon arriving at his apartment door and giving a quick knock, Kayla is greeted by Ian's mother with a fast opening door and a quick, "Hello." Once inside, she is informed that Ian is still in his room and is told, "You are free to go wake him," Ian's mother's instinct tells her he wants a visit from Kayla this morning, since he was away at school for so long.

Kayla makes her way down the hallway, past their kitchen to Ian's bedroom door and as she arrives she begins to knock. She knocks on the door with excitement. She's shouting his name, "Ian! Hello? Ian," Kayla repeats his name with no response.

Ian can make out Kayla calling his name, which wakes him from his dreams.

Ian is at home, waking up in his own bed, thinking what has been happening to him was a dream.

"Ian, how's today treating you, any better than yesterday?" Kayla tries to keep her voice down from the other side of his bedroom door.

"I think so. Come on in," Ian replies to Kayla.

Kayla opens the bedroom door, letting herself in, while Ian wonders if this too is a dream. Ian cannot be sure of anything at this moment.

One thing he is sure of is that each one of his dreams have possibilities of being real to him. Not only in how realistic they are to him, but something has to be connecting the red walls, the bright red apple, the red headphones, and Jax's red bowtie. Is it possible those things happened to him in real life?

"Well, I'm glad you are better today, Ian. You didn't take a moment to open my gift last night," Kayla verbalizes with excitement.

"Oh, you're right! I didn't open your gift. I'm sorry about yesterday. So much has gone on, which we've got to talk about," Ian replies to Kayla.

"We can talk about anything you want to talk about, but only after you open my present," Kayla insists. She is ready to find out what she is giving him. She's been preparing a made-up a story about the gift, but until she can find out what is in the box, she still has some blanks which need to be filled in. She is ready to release this burden off her shoulders and hopes she will be able to make this lie believable to Ian. He's always been able to tell if she is telling a lie just as she is able to with him.

Ian reaches over to his nightstand to retrieve the gift and the card Kayla has given him. Ian is a little surprised Kayla got him a gift, since, in all the years of their friendship, this is the first birthday gift she's ever given him. Ian settles back to open the little box which is wrapped in a smooth, elegant, black paper with a thin white ribbon made into a small bow. Ian thinks the wrapping is too perfect to just rip the box open, but he can tell by the expression of excitement on Kayla's face that she is too excited for him to just open her gift at a slow pace. He begins to rip off the wrapping paper and elegant bow, and starts throwing shredded wrapping paper and ribbon all over his bed. Ian's interpretation of Kayla's expression is exactly how she expected him to open the gift from her.

To Kayla's surprise, once the wrapping paper was removed and the gift was exposed, there was a small red ring box. Now, a ring is not something she is expecting to be in the package, but would fit in the lie she's been making up for the past year. This makes her nerves settle a little, since a ring is something she can work with come story time.

Ian is now holding the small red ring box. *Can this red box also be connected to the red in my dreams?* Ian wonders as he gives Kayla a quick glance of surprise.

"Whatever you're thinking, don't," Kayla half responds to an expression of confusion on Ian's face and trying to make light of the fact she has no clue what is in the box. They both share a short laugh as Ian continues to open the little red box. Kayla is ready for Ian to reveal what "her" gift to him is, which is the final piece of her story to Ian.

Inside the box is a shiny silver ring. Ian is thankful the ring is not a wedding band but a beautiful silver band. Something is written inside the ring, which appears to be Greek, Arabic, or some other language, unknown to Ian. No matter what the language is that is written inside, this is a one of a kind ring.

A silver ring, Kayla thinks.

Kayla watches Ian, as he checks the ring out and she thinks she sees something written on the inside. She is not certain, but as she takes a closer look, the writing does not look like it's in English.

"Where did you ever find this? This is the coolest ring ever!"

Ian is boasting about how the ring is cool, as Kayla is putting the final touches to the lie she is about to tell him.

"I found that ring in a small shop a few weeks ago and thought you might like such a thing for your birthday. And, no, the writing on the inside is a mystery to me as well as to the shopkeeper, so don't ask," Kayla tells Ian in hopes to avoid any questions later.

She tells Ian a story of the shop where she found the ring. Then about the shopkeeper not knowing what the writing meant. *This is easier than I thought.*

I can't believe he only asked where I found the ring, she thinks, starting to relax. She recognizes she will still need to be convincing, or the last year of planning will be for nothing, which means she will let Alexis down and that is not something she is prepared to do.

"Well, go on, make sure the ring fits."

With Kayla's instructions, Ian tries the silver ring on his right hand ring finger. But to his surprise, the ring fit only between the first and second knuckles of his finger. The ring did, however, fit tight over the first knuckle. So the ring is to be worn on his right hand ring finger, over the first knuckle from then on.

"Thank you so much Kayla for this ring. The way the ring fits on my finger is like the way we fit as friends, not the traditional way, but a way that works right for us. This ring is perfect," Ian praises Kayla while reaching towards her to give her a hug.

Kayla leans in to meet Ian's reach for the hug, and as they meet, for just a second, the ring begins to vibrate around his finger. Ian takes this as a sign that Kayla may know something but has not told him yet.

The other possibility is that deep down, Kayla may be holding some information back and not know it. Now is the time to let his friend in on what is going on and find out if she knows anything or has heard anything that she can add.

Now that Ian has opened her gift, this is the time he tells Kayla about his events from yesterday. Now that Kayla's burden has been lifted, by giving Ian the gift from Alexis, she is ready to listen to his day.

***

Ian fills Kayla in on what is going on with him which allows him to relax a little on the inside. He is fine with his decision to leave out a few minor details for now, but the weird expression on her face gives Ian some concern.

Kayla cannot believe what Ian tells her, even as she is repeating the events back to him. *How in the world can he forget about being away at a different school, away from me, for an entire year?* She thinks in amazement. *This is the first time we have ever been apart, and yet he doesn't remember? This is not fair, because I have to remember it!* Kayla's thoughts are starting to hurt her.

Ian suspects Kayla is hiding more than she is revealing, but he is not sure what, or if, it is connected to anything with what he is going through. So Ian does not press the issue with Kayla, for now.

"Okay, so you're telling me that yesterday you woke up on your seventeenth birthday. Then you ate breakfast and went to your room to get dressed for a surprise from your parents. After that, you came back into the living room only to find your parents missing. You decided to head to Central Park to search for your parents, you hailed a taxi, but before you could cross over the Manhattan Bridge, you were heading home from the park in a different taxi. You thought that only a few hours may be missing from your memory, until you got home and realized that yesterday, was your eighteenth birthday instead of your seventeenth birthday." Kayla recaps what Ian just told her. "You went to bed to rest like your father suggested, and you had some very strange dreams last night. How am I doing so far?" Kayla gives a smart retort to Ian.

"So far, you are right on track," Ian replies. He is surprised at how much Kayla remembers about what he told her.

"Then you find yourself waking up in a room with a huge four post bed, high painted cathedral ceilings, with a couple of sitting chairs on a rug. The walls of the room are covered with red wallpaper and what may be family paintings. Oh, and the wood burning fireplace was painted white with gold trim on the mantel. The only light in the room, from what you were able to make out, was coming from a huge candle chandelier which hung from the ceiling, right?" Kayla continues on to the next dream.

"Then, instead of waking up from sleep, you are someplace else now. You now find yourself sitting at an old school desk in an old schoolhouse, right? You can tell it's an old school classroom because of the old wood desk you are sitting at is made to seat two students. Also, the old blackboard behind the teacher's desk, at the head of the room, is not used in today's schools. No sign of overhead lighting in this room either, instead oil lamps are sitting on the shelves, there's an old school world globe, and a piano in the room. You mentioned a wood burning stove for heat, which in today's world is nothing short of a complete fire hazard." Kayla relays back. From the facial expression she gives Ian, she is only making a statement. "Then, just as you are about to head over to the old piano, you hear two boys arguing outside. You, being nosey and clumsy, head over to the window, but before you can make it to the window, you end up kicking over the globe. The bang of the wooden earth hitting the hardwood floors is loud enough for the boys outside to hear and then, instead of arguing, they start yelling at you inside the classroom, but before you are able to peek out at the boys, you are gone again?

Now, you say you are sitting on a park bench in Central Park near Belvedere Castle, alone, then as you are about to make a move to leave, a jogger sits beside you, so you stay seated. The jogger has red headphones around his neck, and is wearing full on jogging gear, but since the jogger does not speak to you, you begin to rise off the bench, and that's when he grabs your wrist calling you by name. He asks you about what birthday you are having yesterday, your seventeenth or eighteenth birthday. He introduces himself as 'Jax' and claims you met him last year on your seventeenth birthday, and he is a teacher at a private school, and your parents want you to meet him. He tells you the watch your parents gave you last year for your birthday has been in your family for many generations. He tells you that the watch holds unique powers, which you somehow access last year, causing your memory loss for the past year. He tells you the dreams you are having are not dreams, but in reality, memories stored in the 'Time Keeper', the watch your parents gave you last year. 'Jax' says he has more to tell you, but he could not tell you then, because time was about to run out of time. Then, just as he predicted, the memory did change," Kayla completes with the first three dreams, or as she learns, memories.

Kayla's facial expression conveys to Ian she needs a break from the recap of the events of his dreams from last night. Ian takes her facial expression of needing a break, but he can sense

Kayla's more knowledgeable about these dreams than he is. Ian cannot say what, but the tone in Kayla's voice, in the way she repeats the dreams to him, reveals to him a sense of hearing about them before, but she is trying to act if this is all new to her. Kayla and Ian grew up together long enough for him to recognize the small things like this about her. Ian decides to play along, because he might learn more about what is happening if he does not let Kayla in on what he's really thinking.

"Okay, where was I?" Kayla's ready to finish with the last of Ian's dreams.

"You are about to finish with the last dream, the one about the party," Ian reminds Kayla, but felt no need in reminding her where she left off if his intuition is correct.

"Oh yes, the last dream you are at a party in a penthouse, on the top of a building in Manhattan, which is an adult party, overlooking Central Park, with a view of Belvedere Castle. At first you don't recognize anyone there, that is, until you come across the man from the park dream. I believe you said his name is 'Jax', except this time he is in a tuxedo with a red bow tie instead of a tracksuit. Then, before you can go speak to him, you glance down to check the time, but you freak-out when the 'Time Keeper' is gone and you are unable to venture over to 'Jax', because then you are awakened by me knocking on your door. Does that about sum things up?" Kayla finishes up.

"Did I leave anything out?" Kayla wants to make sure she completes Ian's dreams.

"You left out the red apple sitting on the teacher's desk in the second dream, but an apple is just an apple," Ian answers. "So what do you make of this?"

"I can't even begin to understand how to start, much less answer 'what do I make of this'. First let me process this for a few minutes," Kayla replies.

Ian shoots back with a quiet, "Sorry, go ahead, process."

After a few minutes of processing the information, Kayla turns her head to Ian, "You can't remember anything for the past twelve months?"

Ian answers, with an exhausted, "No."

Kayla can tell by the way Ian answers that he is telling her the truth. She is afraid to tell him that she has not seen him in the past few months. She is aware of him spending his senior year at a private school but does not want to be the one to tell Ian though.

"Have you had a chance to ask your parents about any of this?" Kayla believes his parents should tell him about the private school he has been attending for the past year.

"No, not yet, because when I walked into the house last night was the first time I had seen either of my parents since yesterday morning. Ever since I walked in the door last night, everything's been a whirlwind. My surprise birthday party, all the guests, the missing time with so many questions, I did not speak to them about this yet," Ian remarks to Kayla.

"Well, I think you should speak to your parents first. They may be able to fill in some of those memory gaps you have, but they are not the last people you saw before losing your memory. I don't think you will be able to find the taxi driver though. You remember, the one who drove you to Central Park last year to search for your parents, since he is the last person you can remember seeing before the memory loss," Kayla tells Ian. She is thinking this will relieve her of telling him the things she does know about him being gone for the past twelve months.

"You may be right, Kayla. I still need to find out where my parents went last year, because when I finished getting dressed and came out of my bedroom, they were missing. Are you going to be around later this evening?" Ian hopes Kayla will be. Ian still wants to talk more about what is happening, and since they grew up together, he's got a notion she is holding something back. But for now, Ian will let the moment go until he speaks to his parents and he finds out more himself.

"Yes, I'll be around. Give me a call, or text, after you find out what your parents say," Kayla assures him.

Kayla stands up and makes her way to the bedroom door and begins to walk out of his room. She glances back and gives an expression of disbelief that this is happening to her best friend. "I wish I was more help to you," Kayla expresses to Ian. She turns and starts walking again. He still thinks she's not told him everything she knows, which is eating him up inside. Ian decides he will not wait until speaking to his parents first, because he needs to find out from Kayla first. Now is the time to force Kayla's hand and find out what she is holding back.

"Kayla, before you go can I ask you a few questions?" Ian pushes to find out what Kayla is holding back.

"Sure, but what about? I can't stay much longer. I'm supposed to go shopping with my mom in a few minutes. I just wanted to come by to check on you. Can this wait until later?" Kayla replies, as she is trying to avoid his questions.

"What are you not telling me? We've been best friends our entire lives, Kayla. I can tell when you are hiding something, or lying, like you are now. You speak of my dreams in such detail, like you are more familiar with them than I am. I feel you are hiding something. What are you holding back and why?" Ian pleads with Kayla.

Crap, he figured out I was lying about where I got the ring. I knew he would tell I lied, Kayla is freaking out in her mind. That is when she hears him say something about her knowing more about his dreams than he does. Kayla is in shock hearing those words come out of Ian's mouth. *What did he say?*

"Ian, what you are talking about? This is my first time hearing any of this. Why would you think any different?" Kayla inquires in return.

"Well, the first mistake you made was the way you repeated my dreams to me. You recited them to me as if that was not the first time you had told them. I can tell when you repeat a story more than once. Remember, we lied to our parents before, so I can tell what a rehearsed line from you sounds like.

The second mistake you made, which I believe you did on purpose, was leaving out the red apple that sat on the teacher's desk in the second dream. I am not sure about why you wanted to leave that part out yet, but I'm sure I will figure that out sooner or later.

Any idea of your final mistake during the recount of my last dream was? Your final mistake was when you called the watch, the one my parents gave me last year which was missing during the party event, the 'Time Keeper'." Ian is straightforward with Kayla, because he wants answers.

Kayla jolts up in shock. *How can he think these things about me?* She asks herself, as Ian is finishing.

"So, because I did not recall your dreams back to you word for word, and I left out a detail or two, I must be more knowledgeable about what you are talking about? Something's gotten into you Ian. I am unsure of what, but accusing me of something like this is not fair to me. How in the world could I be able to know more information about anything to do with you? I think I should leave before you say something else to offend me," are her tearful words as she walks through his bedroom door.

Ian asks another question, before the bedroom door closes. This time he is asking about the gift she gave him, at Alexis' request of course, and the box the ring it is in.

"Is there anything you can tell me about the gift you gave me, this silver ring? You have never given me anything for my birthday before, so why now? Why for my eighteenth birthday and most of all why in this red box?"

I should have thought about the fact that we have never exchanged gifts before. How was I so stupid? Of course he would suspect something about a gift from me. Now, if I had taken that into account, he would not be asking now. Kayla is beating herself up inside for such a small oversight. She decides, instead of having to create more lies, to not answer those questions. She decides to leave him with something simple, yet meaningful.

Ian makes out Kayla's voice before the door is able to close all the way, "It's just a ring Ian. You can wear the ring or not, but I hope you do." Those are Kayla's last words to Ian as she walks down the hall and out of his apartment. She does mean the last part and hopes he will wear the ring because of how much Alexis went through in order for her to give the ring to Ian. Alexis would want him to wear it, even if he never found out who Alexis was, Kayla would know.

Ian still thinks she is holding something back, but he is sure she's doing so for a good reason. He trusts she would help if she could.

Ian is at the point he should tell his parents about what is going on with him and to find out what they know about where he has been for the past year.

Chapter 7

Do My Parents Really Know

After Kayla leaves, Ian knows he needs to pull himself together, get up, and out of bed if he wants to find any answers. He hates when the two of them fight, even knowing they will get past it. Ian returns his focus on the matter at hand. Today, Ian wants to find out what his parents know, and if what they may know may shed some light on, if anything, about what is going on with him, his memory loss, and his dreams.

Ian slips off the silver ring, the gift Kayla had given him for his birthday, setting it on the dresser next to the watch his parents had given him last year. Ian needed to take a quick shower, so he gathers his clothes and heads down the hall to the bathroom. Ian hopes he can grab a shower before anything else strange happens to him.

***

Kayla is walking into her apartment, after walking down from Ian's apartment and being insulted by him. Her mother is awaiting her return for their girl's day.

"It's about time. I was beginning to think you were trying to back out of going shopping with me. I understand you missing Ian, but we've never been on a girls' day," Kayla thinks her mother is being a little over dramatic.

"I'm sorry mother. I did not plan on taking so long up at Ian's. If you allow me a few minutes to freshen up before we head out into public, that would be great," Kayla requests of her mother. "I'll be quick, I promise."

"Fine. You realize what this means? This means that I'm picking where we eat lunch today," her mother replies with a small laugh, as she recalls a place Kayla does not agree with, but she enjoys.

Kayla gives her mom a quick expression of, "OMG," and rolls her eyes with an "okay", turns around and heads down the hall to her room. Their plans were pre-made of going shopping all day, so she had picked out her outfit and hung it on the closet door last night. She snatches the hangers off the door and goes into her bathroom, still not believing she agreed to let her mother pick where they eat lunch for the day. Kayla is in no need of a shower, so she changes into her pre-picked outfit. Once her clothes are changed, she wants to make a few adjustments to her hair and makeup. With the knowledge she is going to be doing a lot of walking for their 'girls' day', she has pre-planned on her hair going up in a ponytail. As far as her makeup is concerned, she figures anything more than a little blush and lipstick will be a mistake. She knows she will end up looking like a crying clown by the end of the day from the sweat caused by the heat of the day.

***

Ian takes his shower with no incident, dries himself off, and puts on the clothes he took with him to wear for the day. Once he dresses, Ian grabs his hand towel to clear off the steam from the bathroom mirror so he can brush his teeth and fix his hair. Ian wants to make sure his appearance is his best for whatever his parents will tell him about his memory loss. He's got to be prepared, because they may not be able to answer any of his questions. Ian will be disappointed if his parents are unable to reveal anything about what is going on with him, but either way, he wants to make sure he is dressed well.

Now that Ian is dressed, he gathers up his dirty clothes and towel and makes his way back down the hall to his bedroom. Once Ian gets back to his room, he puts his dirty clothes and towel in the hamper, walks over to the dresser to put on the last of the accessories he needs to complete his outfit. Ian reaches over and picks up the gift his parents gave him last year, fastening the watch around his wrist tight while checking the time. That's when he realizes he's overslept this morning, and perhaps that is why Kayla came and woke him up.

After the watch is secure on his wrist, Ian reaches over and picks up the silver ring, the gift from Kayla. Ian slides the ring on his finger, just over his first knuckle on his right hand ring finger. At this moment, the watch and ring begin to vibrate, and then memories rush through his mind. The memories hit Ian so fast and hard, he reaches out to grab ahold of the dresser to keep from falling over. Ian is holding the dresser to give him a sense of security and balance, then he closes his eyes and tries to focus on the flash of memories rushing through his mind. Ian is unable to concentrate and focus on any one of the memories in particular and is perplexed when he realizes the memories are going backwards!

***

Now, Ian gets to go home in time for his birthday.

Ian finishes his senior year.

Ian does have a summer break at school.

Ian continues with his second semester.

Ian goes back to school.

Ian comes home for winter break.

Ian leaves for school and attends his first semester.

Kayla?

***

Kayla starts to apply her lipstick looking into the mirror. She can see the small watch on the necklace Alexis had given her start working.

Kayla drops the tube of lipstick down in the bathroom sink to take ahold of the watch and get a better view of it. This is when she sees the clock was not only working, but she notices its tiny hands are moving fast and backwards. Kayla does not have a chance to prepare herself for what is coming next. The next thing Kayla can tell is the bathroom begins filling with rushing wind, wind coming from every direction, not only coming from the direction of the walls but also from the floor and ceiling. With so much wind all around her, Kayla reaches out and grabs the bathroom sink, as she fears she is going to be blown out of the bathroom. "What is happening?" she screams! "MOM!" she shouts again. Kayla knows she would be unable to react to a reply, if her mother is even able to hear her, over the sound of the wind. The fear is close to consuming her of not knowing how much longer she can hold on to the bathroom sink, or what is happening to her mother in the other room. Kayla is unable to correct herself before the sink is yanked out of her grasp and she is twirling through the air in every direction, until she passes out.

To Ian, this overwhelming rush of backwards memories seems to last for a long time. But just like they started, as a rush, they stopped just as fast. Ian cannot remember anything specific about any one of the memories he viewed in reverse, and he does not understand why he saw them.

Ian takes a deep breath, opens his eyes, makes sure he is still balanced, and then let's go of the dresser. To Ian's surprise, though he's still a little lightheaded, he does not fall over after letting go of the dresser. Ian takes a moment to collect himself, scans around his room, but nothing appears to be out of place or any different than before the flash of memories. He does not sense time has changed, not this time anyway. Ian takes another moment to compose himself and hopes time did not change, before he leaves his room.

Ian heads down the hall towards the kitchen where his mother is cooking lunch. Ian enters the kitchen as his mother gives him a smirk with a, "You're up late this morning son. But I guess you are allowed to sleep late since today's your birthday, so Happy Birthday Ian!"

"Morning, and what did you just say?" Ian replies with a sound of shock in his tone.

"I said, 'Happy Birthday'," replies Ian's mother. "One year older and you already forgot today is your birthday?"

"Today's my birthday?"

"Of course it is. What's gotten into you? Are you not feeling well this morning?"

"Nothing's gotten into me, and I'm feeling fine," Ian shoots back. "I must still be waking up."

"Are you sure Ian? If not, I can call Dr. Allen and schedule an appointment for today," Ian's mother replies back to him with the usual motherly concern.

"No. I said I'm fine, but we do need to talk," sounding nervous as he is speaking to his mother. He is half scared and half downright nervous or determined or hesitant to find out what she may tell him. He is not sure if he is ready for the answers she may give him.

"Well, why don't you take a seat at the table so I can finish cooking lunch, and then we can sit and eat a splendid meal together? Your father and I have planned a surprise for you today for your birthday."

With no other questions or comments for his mother, Ian turns and walks into the dining room. Ian crosses into the room, walks over to the table, pulls back a chair from the table and takes a seat. He's more confused now than before he walked out of his room. He is now about to repeat his third birthday in only two days, except he does not recall which birthday he is having today. Just yesterday he woke up to celebrate his seventeenth birthday, then he left to search for his parents only to return home to find out he was celebrating his eighteenth birthday. That was enough birthdays for one day, as Ian made clear when he freaked out a little during his eighteenth birthday party last night. That was why he went to his room in the first place last night, to get some rest as his father had suggested. Now he is waking up to yet another birthday?

While Ian sits at the table waiting on his mother to bring out lunch, he thinks the best thing for him to do is let her bring up which birthday he is having today. Ian tries to keep himself calm by telling himself, *I bet everything was just a dream last night.*

After lunch, I will run down to Kayla's apartment and ask if she remembers giving me this ring at least, Ian thinks as he is waiting for lunch.

Ian does not have to wait long for his mother to bring their lunch to the table. She brings a serving plate of salmon cakes, a bowl of macaroni and cheese, and a bowl of sweet peas, which are Ian's favorites. After she sets the food down in the center of the table, she turns back to the kitchen to retrieve their place settings while asking Ian if he wouldn't mind fetching the pitcher of tea from the refrigerator. Ian does as his mother asks and fills their glasses with ice, before filling them with tea. They both return to the table at the same time, take their seats, and bow their heads to say grace. After they say grace, they make their plates of salmon, mac & cheese, and sweet peas. To Ian this is perfect, because no matter how confusing today is for him, the one thing he is certain about is his hunger. He cannot remember the last time he ate anything.

"Why did you only put place settings for the two of us? Where is Dad?" Ian is having a flashback to waking up and finding his parents missing.

"He ran into town this morning, but he will be here this evening. Don't worry. He would not miss your birthday for anything in the world. You only turn seventeen once, right?" Ian's mother assures Ian.

"I'm seventeen today? That's right, I only turn seventeen once, so he better not miss my party," he senses he is over stating which birthday he is having to his mother, but she does not say anything. Now that Ian understands which birthday he is having, he can assume the rest *was* a dream. Ian is now able to relax, which makes him a little more hungry and able to eat even more of the delicious lunch his mother has prepared.

"So, what is this surprise you and Dad have planned for me," trying to find out information from his mother, who is unaware of what he is up to.

"Wait until your father gets home to find out," she replies. "Now, what do you want to talk about?"

"Oh, nothing important. I was just wondering if you remembered today is my birthday," Ian chooses not to ask his mother anything about what he's now convinced are dreams.

"Okay, if you say so," she replies back. "Where did you find that watch? It looks like an expensive watch."

For a moment, Ian thinks his mother is joking, but then he realizes she is not joking at all. *Does she not remember giving me this watch for my birthday?* Ian is wondering. *How* **can** *she remember? How will my parents be able to buy something for me if I'm wearing it already?*

Right then, Ian is certain something is wrong. Something is going on, not only with him, but also with his mother. He remains silent about what's been happening to him. Ian now confirmed he had not been dreaming, and he is on his own to figure it all out.

"Oh, I found this watch in the back of the cab I came home in last night. What do you think?" Ian came up with a cover story quickly, hoping not to sound scared. He had to think of something quick, since she's not going to be giving him the watch for this seventeenth birthday.

"Sure, but something as expensive as that looks should be returned to its owner, don't you think?" replies his mother.

"You are correct. I'm going to go down to the Taxi and Limousine Commission in New York, and turn the watch in. I'm sure the owner has already made contact with the TLC by now, asking if anyone has turned in a watch by now. Thanks mom for the best birthday breakfast ever, and I will be home later. BYE!" Ian yells as he runs out of the apartment before the door can close behind him.

Ian's mind is flooding with more questions about what is going on with him. He does not understand what could be the cause of this and he wants answers.

Ian can think of only one person to turn to in a crisis like this and that is Kayla. Even after the argument they had this morning; Ian is always able to go to her for anything at any time. Ian makes his way down the hall, into the stairwell, and down to the next floor where Kayla lives. He hopes she has not left to go shopping with her mother yet and is still at home. Ian makes his way down to Kayla's floor, exits the stairwell and heads down the long hallway to Kayla's apartment. Ian gets to her door, takes a deep breath and knocks.

Ian waits for a minute and knocks again. He is about to knock again, *please be home*, as the door swings open. Ian was expecting Kayla's mother to answer the door, but to his surprise, it was opened by a stranger. *Who in the world is this woman?*

"May I help you?" inquires the stranger from inside Kayla's apartment.

"Um, well, is Kayla home?" Ian stumbles out his words to the stranger.

"Who?" Is the reply from the woman.

"Kayla, the girl who lives here," Ian is certain this is where she lives. He's been here many times, since they have lived in the same building their entire lives growing up together.

"I'm sorry, but you must be at the wrong apartment, no one with that name lives here. My husband and I moved in here some twenty years ago. We've seen you and your parents around the building for years, but we've never met. Are you sure you are on the correct floor?" finishes up the neighbor.

"To be honest, I'm not too sure about anything today. I'm sorry if I disturbed you," Ian expresses his apologies as he turns around and starts his way back down the long hallway and back into the stairwell.

How can it be possible my mother has forgot giving me this watch, and how is it possible Kayla does not live in her apartment? Ian is thinking, as he stands in the stairwell. *I'm on my own to find out what is happening to me. I am not sure who I can trust,* Ian thinks as he goes down the stairs to the sidewalk in front of his apartment building.

Ian is thinking of anyone he can turn to now for help. The one person that comes to his mind this time is "Jax", the man in the tracksuit from his dreams. Ian at least has a lead to where he's got to go to find some answers. He also recalls several obstacles will be in his way before he can find "Jax" in the park. One obstacle is getting into the city and another is finding "Jax's'" exact location, that's if "Jax" does actually exist. Ian is not sure of anything at the moment.

I must do a few things first. I need to find another way into the city. Ian worries he may lose, or gain, another year of his life if he tries taking a taxi again. He needs to think for a minute for another way to make his way to Central Park.

***

Kayla slowly begins to open her eyes as a sense of pure calmness washes over. She is able to open her eyes, but she is unable to make out anything around her or to move her body. Yet she still feels calm. "Hello? Is anyone here?" No reply. Even though she can tell she is saying the words, she is not sure if they are coming out of her mouth or if she is thinking them. Kayla does not understand how she wakes up in the condition she is in and still feel so calm, but she does. Even with the knowledge of not knowing where she is, what all's been happening to her, not knowing if her mother is okay, or without even being able to move her body, she is calm. Kayla knows everything in her says she should be scared to death, but she has no fear in her.

"Kayla, you may not understand what is going on now, but trust me when I say you are safe," a familiar voice speaks to her.

"Alexis? Is that you?" Kayla suspects. "What happened, and where are we?"

"You will have time for questions later. For the time being, I have a few things I need to tell you first. Once you accept what I have to tell you, most of your questions may be answered, and you will understand a little better. So, will you allow me to tell you some things first?" Alexis tries to make Kayla feel more comfortable.

"Yes, of course, and I do trust you. Please, tell me," Kayla whispers back.

"Now, some parts of the information I am about to tell you will be hard for you to believe, or understand, but please let me finish. I promise, everything I am about to tell you is the truth. Believe me when I say, this may not be your truth at this moment, but it will be your truth later on in time if history is not changed," Alexis tells Kayla. She is preparing her for what she is about to be told.

"You and Ian inherited a unique bond, a connection, nothing like what's between normal friends, which we will discuss in more detail a little later. You will be told a few more surprises about Ian, but to be fair, he is not aware of these surprises either, not yet. Well, he did not find out about them until he put on the ring you gave him. He will now be able to find out, so 'Thank You' again for keeping true to the promise you made to me a year ago. I also want to thank you for wearing the necklace I gave you as well. Those two things were the most important pieces of the plan, which had to both be completed, or this would not be possible now.

Now, understand I will not be able to tell you everything, but I will tell you everything I can. To begin, let me tell you the life you had is no longer your life. The gift I had you give Ian for his eighteenth birthday was a magical ring, like the necklace I gave you to wear. The ring was designed to erase you from history as if you never existed. The necklace was also designed to keep you in the current timeline, but not in the same way as before. In other words you exist, but you don't. I can tell you that during our first meet in the stairwell in your apartment building, I was not honest with you. I was not visiting Ian the day we met. I was sent to the stairwell to meet you. Now, this is where things are going to become a bit harder for you to believe," Alexis prepares Kayla before continuing.

"Ian being away at school when we met was planned. You being in the stairwell at that very moment was not, let's say, planned, but more as knowledgeable history, because I am not from this time. I was told where you would be that day, at that very moment, by someone that is aware of your whereabouts at every exact moment in time. I came from the future back to the moment we met in the stairwell. You are one of the most important parts of a plan to change the future, which is where I am from. You are a key element that destroys our future, but I believe our future can be changed without erasing you from history. I believe you can, with Ian's help, change your present time, so you can stay in history which will allow you to remain in the future. You need to believe me when I tell you that I am not the only person looking for you, but I am the only one who wants, and needs, you to remain in the future. The others want to use you for their own personal reasons. Those reasons remain to be unknown. The Council is seeking you out to make sure you are wiped from history which will save our future, but it would, in return, destroy all the good which exists in our future because of you. Now, if they succeed in their plan to erase you from history, then they will erase the good you create as well. Now don't worry about that, because the fact that I found you first has changed the future already. At least for the time being." Alexis decides this is enough information for Kayla, for the time being at least.

"Are you alright with everything I have told you so far?"

"I am. But before you go too much farther, may I ask a question?"

"You may ask, but I may not be able to give you a complete answer, or an answer at all, yet. You understand why, don't you?" Alexis replies.

"I do. Now, when you first started preparing me for the information I was about to hear from you, you said that Ian and I have a unique bond, or connection. What do you mean by that?"

"Well, that question I can answer only in part, just not at this moment," Alexis answers, "but in due time."

Robert Starnes

Chapter 8

Back to the City

After thinking of possible routes back into the city, Ian decides on the subway this time. Ian is aware that the subway is not the fastest way into the city but to him anything is better than getting back into a cab. Ian's not only worrying about the possibility of losing time again by taking a cab back into the city but also about having to smell the aroma of the backseat of the cabs and the way the drivers drive through the city. If Ian is to be honest with himself, he worries the most about not finding the answers to the questions he needs for himself. For someone like Ian, searching for an answer to something and being unable to find the answer scares Ian more than anything. Ian is someone who understands that for every equation there is a solution. This situation to him is just another equation which just needs to be solved.

Ian began his walk to Prospect Park from his apartment and began to plan his way into the city. For the residents living in Brooklyn, like Ian who has lived there for his entire life, knowing their way to Prospect Park is second nature just like knowing which subway train will be the best to start his trip into the city. Ian's first stage to getting to the city will start with him getting on the B train. He's got to take the B train to the 81st Street Station and from there he will walk the rest of the way into Central Park. The subway ride to his stop will take him about forty-five minutes to arrive to his destination. The extra time on the subway ride will allow him to try and piece together what's been happening to him. Ian can also think about what, if any of this, may have to do with his dreams, or dream memories.

The subway platform at Prospect Park is not as busy as Ian thought it would be at this time of day. Today being a Sunday, may have something to do with the platform being clear. Many people could be at church. This is not something Ian planned for, so making his first train takes no time at all. With this extra time he is able to board a train sooner than he expected, so he will be ahead of schedule. Ian enters the train, and with the car being almost empty due to the lack of passengers, he is able to find the first available seat and claim it. In Brooklyn when a train is busy or at full capacity, one may find they have to stand for a few stops before an empty seat became available, which is not the case today for Ian.

Ian knows he has twenty minutes before crossing over into the city. Now that he is getting closer to the city, he can't help but think of the last time he tried to go into the city. Ian is going to either succeed this time and find his way into the city, or end up heading back to Brooklyn again. This subway ride will be a long twenty minutes for him for sure. Ian wants to figure out how he went from having his seventeenth birthday to waking up on his eighteenth birthday. He was eighteen for one day and went to bed to wake up on his seventeenth birthday all over again. He also needs to know why this seventeenth birthday is different from the first one. How can his mother not remember giving him his watch, and what happened to Kayla? Why wasn't she in her apartment when he went looking for her?

Ian wants to take advantage of this time to focus on the events which led him up to this point, or back to this point, depending on how he views the situation he is in. Ian tries closing his eyes, resting his head on the back of the subway seat and letting his mind wonder. With a few challenges ahead of him, he knows he has to at least try something, anything. He thinks if he does not try to force the dream memories they will come more natural, but Ian learns that is not going to happen. He is going to try another approach, something he's not thought of before, or thought of before, but not yet. For a few minutes he is unable to block out the noises of the moving train, even with only a few passengers on the car he is on, and he cannot clear up the image in his mind he is able to recall.

No matter how hard he tries, the only things he can remember are from his dreams last night. He cannot help but wonder, *What does a room fit for a King with a red wall, an old classroom with a red apple on the teacher's desk, a man named 'Jax' in the park with red headphones around his neck, then 'Jax' again at an adult party wearing a red bow tie, all have to do with anything?* To top it off, Ian is wondering why Kayla gave him a ring in a red box for his birthday. He's still got so many questions and still no answers. Ian is putting a lot of faith into a man in his dream named "Jax" for the answers to all of these questions.

Ian is certain that at least two events have happened. One is his parents gave him the watch, because he is wearing it. The second is Kayla not only exists, but she gave him the ring he is wearing. Ian needs to find out why his mother forgot about giving the watch to him and why no one remembers Kayla, and where is his best friend now? Ian is now counting on his dreams to be actual memories so at least "Jax" can be real.

"Jax" tells Ian during his third dream, or memory, they met on his seventeenth birthday, which it seems today is his seventeenth birthday, again. So everything now rested on finding "Jax". Ian is not sure what he will do if "Jax" is or is not at the park. On one hand, if "Jax" is at the park, Ian is going to be able to get some answers and at least find out his dreams are real. On the other hand, if "Jax" is not at the park, Ian is back at square one with no leads on what is going on with his mind. But he's at least got to try to find out. His concern right now is making it into the city. Once he makes it over the Manhattan Bridge, he will worry about how he will approach "Jax", if he does find him.

Ian takes a look around at the passengers in the subway car to pass the time, and a young girl sitting with her mother catches his attention. She is around seven or eight and appears to be happy to be going into the city with her mom. Ian wonders if they are headed into the city to shop or to visit someone, anything other than why he is going into the city. He pushes out his reasons for going into the city and thinks more about the mother and daughter. He remembers how he felt when he was younger when his mother would take him into the city. The excitement rushing over him as it did when he was younger. He was so happy.

In the middle of his thoughts, Ian comes back to reality and is now crossing the Manhattan Bridge on the subway. *Here we go,* Ian holds his breath as they are crossing over the river, as he always does when he is apprehensive, hoping he will make it across and not lose any more years or memories this time. The B train crosses over to land as Ian lets out his breath. He's made it into the city. Now, as long as no more surprises spring up, he may find some answers.

Now that Ian is certain he is going to be able to make it to the 81st Street Station without losing any more time or memories, he is able to go back to his previous thoughts. Now he is able to turn his focus away from making it across the Manhattan Bridge, and he is back to wondering why his parents want him to meet this man, "Jax", in the first place. Ian is still questioning whether or not "Jax" is a real person or someone from his dreams, but "Jax" is the only lead Ian's got to go on at this point. The only way Ian is going to find out if any parts of his dreams are real is to at least find out one truth about them. For Ian, finding "Jax" is the only logical dream to prove, or disprove, since it is the only one happening in current time. At this point what's Ian got to lose, because "Jax" will be at the park or he will not. Ian does suspect the only person who can answer his questions is at the park, at least thinks he is at the park, but he has to check for himself.

Now Ian has an understanding of who he is looking for, but he now needs a beginning point to start the search for him. Now, during his dream, the man says he's to wait until his time brought him back. *What does that mean, 'My time to bring me back'? Can this be the reason I'm having my seventeenth birthday again? Can this be what 'Jax' meant by my time bringing me back to him? This must be what he meant. Now, finding 'Jax' is the only thing that will make any sense, and prove if any of the dream memories are real.*

Ian checks the time on his watch to see if the train ride is going to be much longer. He has about ten minutes left before getting off the train, which is perfect for him, because Ian does not like crowds or confined spaces. The closer the train makes its way to the 81st Street Station, the more crowded it became, which is taking Ian back to when he was in middle school. From the start of his middle school years, the older boys would make fun of Ian. The kids would bully him and push him in into his locker, knock him down, call him names, or knock his books out of his hands. This went on for most of his sixth and seventh grade years. Then one evening towards the end of Ian's seventh grade year, the older boys put him in his locker for the last time. This time it was the end of the day, as the other students were going home, and Ian was still stuck in his locker. It was four hours later before the night janitor heard Ian's cries coming from inside his locker. Once Ian was released from his own locker, or personal prison, and his parents were called, he's never been the same in small spaces or crowded places again. After said incident, Ian developed Agoraphobia, an anxiety disorder in which people fear and avoid places that may cause them to panic and a sense of being trapped, helpless or embarrassed. This fear can be an actual fear or anticipated fear of using public transportation, being in open or enclosed spaces, standing in line, or being in a crowd. Ian has not ridden a subway train in some time and has forgotten how many people use it as transportation into the city. *A few more blocks, just a few more blocks,* Ian keeps telling himself.

The train slows down for his stop, and Ian bolts up from his seat and makes his way to the doors. Ian stands at the train doors waiting for the train to stop so the doors will open, as he has an unsettling urge that someone is watching him. He does not want to be obvious, so he begins to scan around the train car through the corners of his eyes. At first no one appears familiar or out of place, but then this girl does. Like a flash Ian turns his head to find a way for a better view at her, but she is gone. For some reason he has a sense about her, but he is unable to find a vantage point with a better view of her to describe her. His view of her was not long enough for Ian to begin to try to place her. *I must be losing my mind*, Ian worries.

Ian shuffles through the crowds of people and then his arm starts vibrating. So far every time his watch, and now his ring, vibrate, something is about to change or did change. Ian is not sure how these things happen, or if he is causing them to happen or why they are happening, but they are happening all the same. "I hope this doesn't stop me from meeting 'Jax' at the park, like I was able to meet him in my dream," Ian says aloud to himself.

Ian exits the train station, while peeking down at his watch and ring, hoping to be able to spot what is causing one of them to vibrate, but the vibration has stopped. *I wonder if this is connected with the girl on the train.* Ian can spot nothing wrong with either his watch or the ring, so he drops his arm back down to his side and continues walking down the sidewalk. When the watch and ring are vibrating, from what Ian's learned, the combination means something. So while he makes his way down the sidewalk, he makes sure to keep his guard up. Ian, unsure of what to expect, is going to have to be vigilant and very aware of his surroundings as he continues to Central Park. The possibilities of a change made in history, either very small or not having anything to do with him or his surroundings, were endless. On the other hand, it could have been something so drastic that it changed the world. Even if things appear the same, it does not mean they are.

Ian continues north on the sidewalk along Central Park West to the 81st Street crosswalk. He remembers he can enter the park and then walk about fifteen more minutes to Belvedere Castle. Ian may find "Jax" waiting at the castle or may pass him on his way to the castle, which he heads to in any case. It is the only place Ian can think of to start looking for answers.

Ian makes his way across the Central Park West crosswalk, but he cannot help but wonder if all these people are affected by the same thing he is dealing with or even if they are real. *Can this all be a dream? Only time will tell.*

Robert Starnes

Chapter 9

"Jax"

Ian makes his way across the street to the other side of Central Park West and starts his way through the entrance into Central Park. All of a sudden, he's hit with a sense of déjà vu. This is not the usual déjà vu Ian is used to having though. He does not recall being here any time earlier, or the same thing is happening again, but rather more like something will be happening again at another time. The best way Ian can describe this version of déjà vu is like it is the first time of an event which will cause déjà vu to someone in the future.

Ian shakes off the notion and continues on his way through the entrance. Ian knows the way to Belvedere Castle will not be challenging, since his mother had taken him there for many years as a child. She would take him to this castle every Saturday, which was her way for them to share mother and son time together before he grew up. Ian, of course like all children do, has gotten too old to enjoy those moments now. Ian always had a fascination with Central Park and castles. His mother thought Belvedere Castle was the perfect spot for her to take him, since it was located in Central Park. She would spend hours and hours at the park with Ian. For the first few years she would push him in his stroller, showing him the animals, the trees, and the castle, of course. As the years went on, Ian grew out of the stroller and would walk alongside his mother on their walks. Ian was always inquisitive about nature and history. He would also ask his mother about the history of Belvedere Castle and Central Park. It was as if he could never get enough information. They were never too far away from the castle. So, as many times as he's been to Belvedere Castle as a child, forgetting the way there was impossible for Ian.

Ian remembers there are two paths which will lead to Belvedere Castle. He recalls one of the paths is shorter than the other, but it takes a little more time to complete as that path is meant for walkers. The other path is a bit longer, except it is quicker to complete if you are in shape as that path is meant for runners or joggers. He chooses the shortest walking path, the one meant for walkers, from the street that lead towards the castle. The reason he chooses the shortest path, even though it takes longer, is because he is in no mood to relive his glory days of track as a freshman. Ian is remembering his parents' insistence of his participation in some type of sports while in high school. They had some preconceptions that if Ian was in some type of sport he would make more friends. After taking into consideration his intelligence and thin frame, they thought track and field would better suit him than football or any other contact sport. Ian only participated in track for a year, not just to please his parents, but to see for himself if it could do it. The next year he told them, straight up, that he was not going to be part of the track team. He gave them an excuse that he wanted to focus more on his academics because if he was going to be applying for scholarships for college, that's where he would more likely be able to receive one. They all knew an athletic scholarship was not looking promising for him.

Ian continues down the park walking path still trying to recall some of his memories, while getting distracted by all the people in the park around him. Ian finds himself watching all the families walking the path he chose. Among the families at the park, there are some two parent families, some with moms and dads, and others with either two dads or two moms pushing strollers, while some single parent families doing the same. Not all the parents are pushing strollers, since some of their children are old enough to walk, so they are holding their hands instead. The families with more than one child are the ones which drew Ian's attention the most. Ian, being an only child, often wonders what life would've been like growing up with siblings. Ian witnesses two dads walking with their two children, laughing, playing games, holding hands and having genuine fun. He is so wrapped up in watching them, he almost didn't recognize his own name being called. Then he hears someone calling his name again, so he scans around the park and recognizes the man from his dreams, "Jax", dressed in the exact same track suit, running shoes, and the same red headphones around his neck. Ian is in shock, by the way "Jax" is dressed and it matches his dream, exactly. This makes Ian question whether or not he is in a dream, or is THIS déjà vu. *What is going on with my dreams? Is this what the real meaning of déjà vu is, or can I be psychic?* He let those thoughts go for the time being, so he could focus on the task at hand. Now Ian might be able to find some answers to some of his questions. At least he hopes this is the person who can give him some of the answers to some of the questions about what has been happening to him.

Ian starts towards the man in the track suit. He's hoping this is the "Jax" from his dream, and then recognizes the park bench between them. Ian remembers in his dream he is sitting on a bench talking to "Jax". He thinks, *Why not?* Ian walks over to the park bench while the other man is coming towards him. Ian takes a seat on the bench, while the man in the track suit strolls up and stands beside the bench. The man Ian suspects is "Jax", stands there for a moment taking in the surroundings. Ian is not sure what the man is looking at, or looking for, but Ian is sure he does not want to disturb him.

After the man from his dreams, in the track suit, referred to as "Jax", finishes looking around, he takes a seat on the park bench beside Ian. Ian takes a deep breath, because this is the moment he's been waiting for. This will be the moment of truth for him. This will determine if everything leading Ian to this moment in time is real or was a dream. This is the moment when Ian will learn the true name of the man from his dreams. This is the man in the track suit, the man he's been calling "Jax", or this man is about to ask him for directions or the time. If anything is going to begin to piece together any of Ian's past few days, past year, or last night, this is the time. *"Jax" has to be here to help answer my questions. He just has to be.*

Ian did not realize it, but he is holding his breath like he did before on the train. He does this whenever he is nervous or apprehensive. He is unsure what to expect, for the next few minutes, from "Jax". Will he find out any answers, or will he be left with more questions? This is so surreal to him, and then the man turns to Ian, and his suspicions are confirmed with one introduction. The man in the tracksuit speaks, "Hello Ian, my name is Jax. This is going to sound strange to you, but I first met you yesterday on your seventeenth birthday. Now, I know that today's your seventeenth, which means yesterday's today." Jax tells Ian. "Stop me if you are having a hard time keeping up with what I'm telling you."

Ian is unable to reply at first, until he lets out the breath he's been holding and is able to relax, because now he's found his starting point. Now he is certain his "dreams" are real, and "Jax" is real. Knowing that he is not alone in what is going on in his life makes him feel more at ease.

"Yes, I had a dream last night in which you told me about our first meeting. I don't remember the actual meeting, but you do, don't you?" Ian spouts out without skipping a beat. "How is it that you are so acquainted with who I am, and yet, I cannot recall ever meeting you? How could you believe we would meet twice? There is something going on with me, and I have no clue what's happening. You are the only person I feel that I can turn to during all of this, and that is only because I saw you in my dreams. Is there something wrong with me? Because if the only person I can turn to during a time of need, is someone I have only seen in my dreams, then what?"

"No Ian, there is nothing wrong with you."

Now that Ian is able to get that off his chest and get it cleared up, he is now ready to get answers to the questions he really has. Questions like finding out how much knowledge Jax has about his watch, and if Jax can reveal anything about Kayla, or about the ring she gave him, even though she won't give the ring to him until next year, for his eighteenth birthday. *Where does the ring come from, if Kayla does not exist now?* Ian wonders to himself before he questions Jax. "Yesterday, my parents gave me this watch for my birthday and today my mother does not recognize it. I understand, since today is my first seventeenth birthday, she has not actually given me a gift yet, but I am still wearing the watch anyway. So, it was given to me at some point in time, by someone. Correct? Then you come along and tell me, in my memory dream, this watch has been in my family for many generations. So again, if that is true, then why did she not recognize it as the Time Keeper, at least, this morning?"

Jax takes a slow and steady breath as he can tell this will take some time to explain. He also realizes he has plenty of time to explain it since he's explained it to Ian once before. At least he thinks he did.

"You may remember some of what I'm about to tell you, so please stop me at any time if you recall something that I have already told you. Okay, now let's start with something simple, shall we? It seems as though I did mention some facts about the watch to you, the one your parents gave you yesterday, being in your family for generations, but did I mention the watch has powers and ..." Jax is unable to finish his first sentence before Ian chimes in.

"Let me stop you there real quick, Jax. You did explain this part to me in my memory dream. You told me about the watch's power to store memories, and that the watch is called the Time Keeper, and that I will be able to access the Time Keeper, next year, once I turn eighteen. Now, you were unable to tell me anymore details about the Time Keeper, because you said the memory I was accessing was about to change, and just as like you said, the memory changed. So let's skip to the part after you tell me about the watch's powers, you know, when you ran out of time last time. I would say you can start there," Ian is, more or less, telling Jax than asking. "Again, if the Time Keeper's been in my family for generations, then why didn't my mother recognize it this morning?"

"Well, since you are wearing the watch today, that would mean they were unable to purchase the watch for you this time for your seventeenth birthday as a gift and maybe why she didn't recognize it. We can come back to this later, but right now we need to find out exactly when your memories ended. Now, your memories changed yesterday right after you came here looking for your parents after your first seventeenth birthday, right? Well, I can tell you that I met you here and explained the watch, or the Time Keeper, to you, which must be why you are having your seventeenth birthday repeated for a second time. You found a way to access this memory you stored in the Time Keeper and are changing your past. I have a question for you, where your parents missing this morning before you left the apartment to come here?"

"No. Well, my mother is home, but my father is not there. My mother said he's in the city doing something, but he will be home in time for my birthday party," Ian replies.

"Then this must be our true time to meet. Can you recall any other changes? They can be either major or minor," Jax questions Ian.

"Are you kidding me right now? You want me to tell you if I can tell if I can recall anything different right now, either major or minor? What can be possibly be bigger than going back in time and having my seventeenth birthday repeated?" Ian exclaims.

Jax gives Ian an expression, which means for him to continue, so he does.

"Well, for my eighteenth birthday, my best friend Kayla gives me this ring I'm wearing," showing Jax the ring Kayla gave him. "What is odd about this is that in our entire lives we've never exchanged gifts before for our birthdays. Then after my mom does not recognize the Time Keeper this morning, I thought Kayla would be able to tell me something about last night. So I told my mom I would be back later and left. I went straight down to Kayla's apartment, but when I arrived there someone else answered her door," Ian replies.

"What does this have to do with something changing? Does she always answer the door?"

"No, you don't understand. What I am telling you is that I did not recognize the person who answered the door. Another couple living in her apartment claims the two of them have been living in her apartment for twenty years. It's like she never lived there at all. I'm not even sure if my parents will remember Kayla either. Time's not really been on my side today. Since I left my apartment this morning, last night was the first time I have been back, and that's when I realized I had lost a year. Then I wake up this morning and I am seventeen again. So I am back to where I started, but I do not remember the year I lost to begin with. Do you think my mom will remember Kayla, when she doesn't even remember giving me this watch? Kayla and I grew up together the majority of our lives and went to the same schools. Now she is gone and I don't know where she is or how to find her."

"Well, that is different than just not being at home or answering the door," Jax replies to Ian.

"I will tell you everything else that I know, but first I need you to tell me about the watch my parents gave me for my birthday."

"Okay, but in order for me to tell you about the watch and its powers, I think you first should hear the story about the watch and its history. Is this okay with you?"

"I guess so then, if you must," Ian answers back.

So Jax begins to tell Ian the story of the watch with time lost. The story of the Time Keeper.

Chapter 10

Introducing the Pocket Watch

Jax begins to tell Ian the fascinating history of the creation of the first time piece. Jax cannot continue with the legend of the Time Keeper, until he fully tells the history of the watch. He needs to give Ian the full background of the invention of watches, its entire history, and of the creator himself. He wants to help Ian understand the meaning of the Time Keeper and why he and the watch are so important. So Jax begins with the history of the origin of the watch and its creator.

"The watch first appears in 15th century Europe. Though without evidence, to historians that is, of who first actually created the first watch, it is believed to have been created by Peter Hele which we can confirm to be the truth. In the beginning, the intent of the watch's initial creation was meant to be worn as pendants by women as accessories to their outfits.

Women would continue to wear the pendant watches for several centuries. Then, during the 17th century a chain was added to it, which was called a fob. The fob then made it possible for men to be able to start wearing watches in their pockets without the worry of losing them. You see, one end of the chain was attached to the watch while the other end had a clasp, which they could attach to their jacket allowing the actual watch to be carried in their pockets. Hence the familiar term, 'Pocket Watch', which you hear today.

Again, the watch's initial creator, Peter Hele, did not intend on it being worn by men at that time, and I doubt he intended for it to store memories in it either. History, which you will not read in any of your common history books, later says that Peter Hele not only created the first watch to tell time, but also a way to store time. I would not say he created a way to store time exactly, but a way of storing moments in his life and putting them in a safe place. Those moments, or memories, would be stored until, if and when, he wanted to go back and relive any stored moment. All he would need to do was to access the storage container of those memories. In the beginning, he thought only he had the ability to store and to access his own memories in his creation. He did not realize, until later, that he had created a Time Keeper for his bloodline to access for generations to come. While Peter knew he could access his stored memories, he was not certain he could change those memories. He also was not sure if he changed those memories if they would change his present time, so he never tired. Peter understood the possible repercussions of going back and changing a memory, the possibility that could end up resulting in making it is as if an event never happened in the first place.

It isn't until after his son, Wolfgang Hele, turns eighteen, Peter realizes Wolfgang's ability to access the Time Keeper as well. One night, Wolfgang takes the Time Keeper out from his father's nightstand, and the next thing he knows, he's gaining access to the Time Keeper. He falls hard to the floor immediately in his father's room. He hits the floor so hard that Peter wakes up to find Wolfgang lying unconscious on the floor clutching the Time Keeper tight. Unsure how he should proceed, Peter decides to let time run its course and hope Wolfgang did not change anything by accident. Remember, at this point in time, Peter only knew he could store and access his own memories, so he didn't know what Wolfgang was doing in the Time Keeper. For what felt like an hour to Peter just waiting for his son to snap out of it and wake up, he never left his side. Wolfgang wakes up twenty minutes later with a confused look on his face. Peter finds out that Wolfgang has the ability to access the Time Keeper, and luckily Wolfgang was only able to store a memory of his in it. He was unable to access any of Peter's memories which were stored. This forces Peter to tell him about the Time Keeper and about what a few of the consequences using the Time Keeper could be. He also starts training Wolfgang on using the Time Keeper and to make sure the secrets of the Time Keeper stay away from everyone except their family bloodline. So begins the tales of the Time Keeper, which would only be told to each generation of Hele's family, from generation to generation to come.

From then on, if and when they wanted to, his family bloodline had the ability to access their own stored events and relive them. Now, accessing one's stored events could have resulted in some risky consequences. Now, let's say someone in your family chooses to access one of their events, and they go back and change the outcome of said event, thus causing history to change forever from that moment they selected going forward. You see, the thing about going back in time and messing with history is no one can predict the outcome, which by altering the smallest past event can alter one's current life in the biggest way. For instance, let's say someone went back in time, and they changed something accidentally and without knowing they did. What would you say if I told you that that could end up effecting said event, like for example, it could cause them to take a different path in life? Now, don't take that literally when I say a different path in life, I am simply saying they may have taken a right turn on the sidewalk instead of the left they took in the original memory. Now, they would store that altered memory in the Time Keeper instead of the previous one they went back to in the first place. What if by doing this, it caused them to miss meeting the love of their life. Now that they have not met the love of their life, this could cause some significant effects on the outcome of a person's current timeline, don't you agree? What if they had children? They would not exist in the new timeline. What if they saved someone from being killed, who was important to the future, then that person would have been killed and the future could change for everyone in a very drastic way. Are you following along so far?" Jax questions Ian.

"Yes, I understand how something like that may cause life changing events."

"Even though there were safeguards in place with the Time Keeper, such as the one of only your family bloodline having access to it and only being able to access one's own memories, the effect of changing history is a precautionary tale mentioned as well. With the safeguards in place, it was safe to assume that if the Time Keeper ever became lost, stolen, or given away, then the events stored in it became lost. This came to be known as 'time lost'. It's believed to be true since there are no reports of anyone ever accessing another ancestor's memories during the past centuries. The fail-safe also seems to be put in place to make sure no one was able to go back too far in history, by mistake or on purpose, to try and alter it all together. Can you imagine if someone else had the ability of accessing the Time Keeper and going back to the beginning of the original memories stored in it and changing them? Well, it was a fail-safe, until you came along. We are still not sure how you are able to access another's memories stored in the Time Keeper, but we will help you find out.

As I mentioned before, the Time Keeper is said to have been passed down from generation to generation from the creator, Peter Hele's family, until the mid-19th century. Legend then says that Sebastian Helen, the last of the Hele bloodline on record of possessing the Time Keeper, lost the Time Keeper during a fight with his closest friend, Grayson Zimmerman. The cause of the fight is unclear to this day, but that would be the last time the two of them ever spoke.

Sebastian and Grayson grew up together their entire lives, kind of like the way you and Kayla did. They both lived and grew up in the same small town of Danvers. They spent so much time together that people thought of them as brothers, and they did too. The pair of them, born the only child to their parents, became as close as they did very quickly and naturally. They were always there for each other, which was until after the night of their big fight. Those two had been friends for over thirty years, and some say Sebastian took the loss of their friendship really hard. Grayson is the only person outside of the Hele bloodline that was aware of the existence of the Time Keeper. Sebastian knew that he was not to ever speak to anyone about the Time Keeper or about what it can do. He knew that their family secret must be kept within the family since its creation, and Sebastian's father intended for it to stay a family secret. Unfortunately Sebastian let his guard down as he let Grayson become closer to his heart as their friendship grew. He loved him as his brother and he trusted him, therefore, he felt he earned a right to be told about the Time Keeper. The simple thoughts of children and friends, even though they may not mean harm by their actions, they also may not always know how their actions turn out in the long run later in life.

Sebastian, telling Grayson about the Time Keeper, goes to show you just how much value he placed on their friendship. Like I said before, Sebastian considered Grayson his brother. His feelings compelled him to tell Grayson about his family's history, but he did not feel that compulsion outweighed his obligation to his family because to him Grayson was part of his family. Sebastian was concerned that if anything happened to him it would be a logical choice for Grayson to be the one to continue the Time Keeper's history. Sebastian had been using the Time Keeper over the years to keep their friendship together. He found himself going back in time and changing the outcome of fights they had gotten into the night before. He did so with care though. He was not trying to change anything major that could alter history in any other way than the outcome of their fight or argument.

One night, after a long day of drinking, the best friends ended up in an alley behind the pub where the fight that ended their friendship started. As to why the pair of them began fighting is still a mystery but to hear about the outcome was a heartbreaking moment for Sebastian.

After their fight, Sebastian wanted to store the moment in the Time Keeper, at least until he was able to go back and face something he had done wrong to Grayson and correct it. No one was for certain of what Sebastian did to Grayson, and still to this day, no one is for certain. That's the moment when he realized the Time Keeper was missing. Sebastian, knowing how important the Time Keeper was to his family, went back to the alley where their fight had taken place in hopes of finding it, but to no avail. The Time Keeper was nowhere to be found, nor anywhere around the alley. It was gone, leaving Sebastian without any hope of ever being able to go back and correcting the error of his ways of the evening. Sebastian did not take that loss as the losing of a friend, but in the sense of the pain of losing the life of a brother. Those two had remained friends for over thirty years and for many of those years Sebastian used the Time Keeper to go back and fix anything coming between them. Now, the one time he deemed it truly necessary to store a memory in the Time Keeper and being at the absolute most important moment in his life, he couldn't find it, and there was nothing he could do about it. What's been said and done between Sebastian and Grayson would forever remain the wedge between them. It would keep them from ever becoming friends, or brothers, again. Sebastian would remain heartbroken for the rest of his life.

Sebastian knew the Time Keeper was lost forever and the dangers that the Time Keeper would be in if it fell into the wrong person's hands. So, on Sebastian's death bed, he tells his grandson the story of the Time Keeper, Grayson's knowledge of their family history, their fight, and losing the Time Keeper. After he tells his grandson the stories, Sebastian makes him promise to never stop telling those stories to their family members for generations to come until the time that the Time Keeper is back in possession of the Hele family. His grandson promises to tell the tale to the coming generations and promises to continue the tradition and make sure that the stories are told from generation to generation.

Word of the Time Keeper's existence or its power had not come up for over a century. 'The Time Keeper must have been in a safe place', is what many had thought.

Then one year rumors began surfacing of the possibility of the Time Keeper being in possession of a man named Talbot Wisner. Talbot was a famous and successful businessman in New York City. His company played a huge role in getting many of the buildings we see around us today built. Back then, if you had the means and were able to afford the construction, a building plan and a design, all you needed was to go and see Talbot, and he would make it happen. Talbot was a crude businessman whose reputation was one that made him the type, with his ability, the kind to achieve things no other person was able to achieve. No one understood how he was able to have previously denied permits suddenly approved. He was able to get liquor licenses for some questionable clients which had been denied prior requests. He did this not only for one of their restaurants but for seven of their restaurants and three of their bars. The gossip around the city was that Talbot was able to out think and out plan anyone he went up against. After each failed permit attempt, Talbot was able to learn something important that gave him an advantage to approach the people in charge of the permits at a different angle."

"It wasn't long after Mr. Wisner's death that the rumors stopped. No one ever figured out what happened to the Time Keeper after his death."

Ian could tell that, being a History teacher, Jax loves sharing this story. He tells it with such passion. Passion is what keeps Ian at the edge of the park bench, and that passion is what keeps Ian wanting to hear more.

"Until two years ago, for those of us who've always believed in the Time Keeper, the Believers as we are called, the legends are true for the most part."

"Now, the Believers did not always exist. It was Sebastian's repeat usage of the Time Keeper, going back and repairing his friendship with Grayson, which caused a small group to form within the Council. This group has the ability to sense any changes in history being made each time Sebastian made them. In the beginning they were unsure what to make of these feelings, so the Council did what they did whenever there was a new craft, energy, or other type of power noticeable to them but could not explain at the time. They began to search for the source of what was causing these feelings of change.

The Council is a group that keeps watch over all things unexplained by regular people, and they make connections everywhere all over the world. Their network started growing even faster after the Salem Witch Trials in 1692. Even though over 150 women and men, along with 1-four year old child, from Salem Village and surrounding villages were accused of using witchcraft, only nineteen were executed before the Superior Court of Judicature stepped in to help. Witch's fears grew all over the world, and they vowed to help the Council in any way they could in exchange for any protection they may offer them. With that arrangement made all those years ago and still remaining intact today, the Council was able to find out about the Time Keeper along with its history. In finding out the Time Keeper's history, Sebastian Helen came up as the current Hele family member in possession of the Time Keeper during that period. The group in the Council assumed the responsibility of changes. As they assumed those changes did not affect history in a major way, they deemed it unnecessary to reveal their presence to Sebastian.

Even though they did not take Sebastian as a threat to history, they still wanted to make sure the Time Keeper's powers, and Sebastian, had a watchful eye on them just in case. Each member of the Council who was tied to the Time Keeper and its powers, gave up one of their children to live in the outside world as a Believer. Their purpose is to tell the tale of the Time Keeper, as the Hele family members do, generation to generation. The difference in their tales from the Hele family tales, is that the Believers are told not to interfere unless there is a major history change event happening or about to happen. The Believers are also told to make sure that the Time Keeper remains in the possession of a Hele family bloodline at all times. Just in case, for some reason, if the Time Keeper is ever lost or stolen, they are permitted to help the descendants of Peter Hele during that time period to locate the Time Keeper. The only drawback is only being allowed to help in indirect ways. They are not allowed to approach the current descendant of the Time Keeper at that time period and tell them of its exact location. However, spreading rumors around enough to draw their attention and point their focus in the right direction is allowed.

The Believers were not able to help Sebastian locate the Time Keeper after this fight with Grayson because of the fact the first Believers were children at that time. The Council was just forming the Believers at the time, so the Time Keeper would remain lost until the rumors of Talbot, of course. I will go and take look back through the records to see who the Believers were that were assigned during that time period. I think it may be possible they led Talbot to the Time Keeper, or maybe they gave it to him, especially after the Time Keeper's first appearance after centuries of being missing. Now there are many of us Believers who are teachers at the school. There are Believers of other areas of the Council just as there are many areas of this world not explainable by the natural human being, one would say. We are all essential parts of a larger grand design. We do what we can to make sure that the ones we are here to help receive what they need from us," Jax concludes with the history of the Believers.

"Now, where did I leave off? Oh yes. Up until two years ago, when the news reported a man found murdered over his wrist watch caught our attention, many people thought the murder was a mugging, just a senseless act of cruelty. Then when the police caught the murderer with the watch in his possession, he stated someone had hired him to kill this man and steal his watch. Then the Believers unraveled the truth about the murdered man. He was a descendant of the Hele family bloodline. After the murderer was arrested and the watch was logged as evidence for his trial, the Believers thought the Time Keeper was in very safe hands for the time being. No one figured the watch would go missing only a few short days after the arrest of the murderer."

"When your parents gave you the Time Keeper for the first time, for your first seventeenth birthday, that was when the Believers first felt history change, in a very large way, in a way causing concern to us. History changed the day you put on that watch along with the ring, the ring Kayla gave you on your eighteenth birthday," Jax is pointing at Ian's right hand, where he wore the watch and ring.

"Now, not only do the Believers know it is possible to access the time lost, but that it can only be accessed by a direct descendant of Peter Hele and by you to be exact. The descendants of Grayson now may know this information as well. This is how we think you are here, now, at this time, a year in the past. Your, Great, Great, uncle is Sebastian Helen. He is also who your parents named you after, Sebast-IAN."

"Ian, the reason I am aware of these things is because I am a Believer. I was invited here by your parents to help you understand the powers of the Time Keeper and to teach you how to use them, if, or in case, you ever needed to use them. They also wanted me to show you how, and why, to protect the Time Keeper at all cost. Your parents are aware of the Time Keeper's history, because it was told to your father when he was a child. That's why when he saw the watch in the case at the antique bookstore, when you were having your first seventeenth birthday, he understood the meaning of getting the Time Keeper back. Now, as you can tell, history has changed and, because of that, your father did not buy the watch for you from the antique store. Something more is going on here than accessing the Time Keeper. Something else is going on, and I bet that ring is involved which is why I think you have been sent back to your seventeen birthday. Now the other surprise your parents planned for you, before they went missing, was for us to meet and for you to come with me to our school and train on how to use the Time Keeper," Jax is finishing with the history lesson for Ian.

"You don't remember, but you did come to school with me and train for a year, until you came home and put on the ring from Kayla."

"I'm sure you have plenty of questions, but they'll need to wait for now. Our first priority is for your arrival home and for us to talk to your parents. I'm sure they are worried sick about you, since you are the one who is missing now, instead of them, on your first seventeenth birthday," Jax reminds Ian of the changes in history.

"Okay, Jax fine. I'm going to need a little time to collect my thoughts together, and I'm also tired. Today's been either a very long day, a year, or who can tell, maybe just a long few hours," Ian tells Jax as confusion is starting to cloud his mind.

So the two of them leave the park bench and head to the park exit at 81st Street and Central Park West. Then they will hail a cab to take them to Ian's home where his questions can all be answered in detail, at least Ian hopes they can.

Chapter 11

Red

Ian and Jax are making their way out of the park, and Ian wants to understand more about the Time Keeper. The number of times he has been to Belvedere Castle, from his mother taking him here during his childhood, Ian knows making it to the street exit is going to take some time. Ian decides this is the perfect time to take advantage of the extra time he's got with Jax and thinks he may be able to learn more information from him. So as they continue walking, Ian decides to ask Jax a few questions about the Time Keeper.

"Jax, just how does one store a memory in the Time Keeper to begin with?" Ian sounds clueless. He is not sure if Jax will be able to answer the question, since he is not someone who is able to access the Time Keeper himself. He thinks asking Jax this line of questioning is a great way to find out just what he does know, which will be determined by the answer he receives in return. Ian has an ability to learn great details about someone just by asking questions and the answers they gave in return. If Jax knows more than he lets on, then Ian will be able to tell. Ian wants to find out as much as he can about the Time Keeper, because the more he learns about the Time Keeper the more he learns about himself. Ian needs to uncover as much as possible about himself and the Time Keeper if he wants to be able to begin his search for his best friend Kayla.

"Well, I cannot tell you much except what's been told to me over the years. There have been stories told down through the generations of Believers, but your family's bloodline are the only ones who will be able to answer those types of questions for you. They are the ones who can access the Time Keeper and store memories," Jax replies.

Ian knows Jax is telling him the truth. He had a feeling that was going to be the conclusion to that question, but he had to be sure. He knows he has to try a different approach.

"Well, tell me what's been told to you over the years, since I am a blank slate knowing nothing at all about the Time Keeper or my family history. I can only rely on my experiences and what you have told me so far," Ian demands of Jax.

"I'm sorry Ian, I didn't think of how you may view things. You are at a disadvantage more so than the others who have possessed the Time Keeper before you. Your ancestors before you were at least taught by the ones before them to prepare them. You, on the other hand, have not had the privileges they received. Okay, I will tell you what I have been told over the years as I was growing up. Remember, these are just speculations and I am unsure how accurate they are, if at all.

Now, to store a memory in the Time Keeper, the one who wants to store time must pick something in the memory and focus on it. From what I understand, they are making the object in the memory the focal point to make the memory easier to recall at a later time. Try and think of it like you are putting a label on a file folder and then putting the file folder in a filing cabinet. What do you imagine a filing cabinet would be like if you open it and its files and folders have no labels? Do you think finding a file without a label would take you a long time to find?

The same concept applies here with the Time Keeper and this creates sort of a filing system for your family," Jax explains to Ian.

"How am I going to be able to tell what memories I will want to keep? I won't realize that I need an item to focus on in the memory as it's happening, now will I?" Ian shoots back to Jax. Ian has a quick flashback of being in a class at school and no clue what the subject is or what is going on. *How am I going to be able to recall what I need to remember if I have not been told I need to remember a moment at the time? How can anyone be expected to remember something beforehand,* Ian wonders?

"Okay, slow down Ian. Let's take this one step at a time. First, you don't need to be in the middle of the actual event you want to remember as it is happening. Second, when you recall a memory you want to store in the Time Keeper, that's when you will want to make a focus item. A focal item will be something you can recall during a memory, something you can easily remember. The focal item will become the label for the Time Keeper, for that memory," Jax replies. "Does this answer your question?"

"Well, in a way." Ian is not only wanting to gather as much information as possible about the

Time Keeper, but needs to understand how he is going to be able to use the information. Ian remembers something from school and that's every student stores files on a computer in their own way. Depending on which class they are in, helps determine some part of the way the file is saved. Like, if they are in a history class, they may start out the beginning of the file name with "History 101.Lab 2.3rd period.pdf", at least this way they will be able to find their file, if all the class files are saved on a server. They will be able to find their file saved for their History 101 class, Lab second class, during third period, as a .pdf file on the server. In some cases they may put their initials on the end of the file name, in case everyone may share the same server. "This does answer my question in part, by helping me if I need to find a memory I save in the Time Keeper, but locating a memory stored by someone else in my family bloodline, not so much," Ian protests.

"Well, you did not ask me about how to locate a memory in the Time Keeper. You asked me about how to save a memory in the Time Keeper. So if you are asking me if I have any knowledge of how to use your family's filing system in the Time Keeper, then you have me at a loss. You and your bloodline are the only ones who have ever been able to access the Time Keeper. I am not certain what the items labeled will look like. One thing I have heard is that they will stand out from the rest of the memory, something noticeable. Then again, each family member may work out different ways of storing memories. Remember, until now, accessing others' memories was not possible, or so we thought. Now, is there something or anything you can think of which may stand out in the memories you accessed before you were sent back to being seventeen again?" Jax starts to probe Ian deeper into his memories to find more answers.

Ian is a little skeptical to tell Jax he has already made a connection between the memories, which is that each memory shared something in common, nothing major, but a connection all the same. One thing, at least one thing, in each memory is the color red. *I wonder if the color red can be the sort of thing to be considered as a label that Jax is talking about,* Ian asks himself.

"Well, can you think of anything?" Jax probes Ian last time for any information. "Remember, it can be any detail, no matter how big or small, it just has to be the same, or very close to the same, in each memory," Jax can tell Ian is holding something back, but he does not want to push him too hard. He does not want Ian to shut down, or close himself off, but Jax forces himself to continue with this questioning for Ian's sake, though he may not find the answers he is looking for, not yet.

"Give me a minute, I'm trying to think," Ian is stalling for time as the pair continue walking out of the park. After he debates in his mind for a few more minutes, Ian decides to go ahead and tell Jax the truth. The truth about what he did find out about what each one of the memories have in common. "Well, one thing comes to mind in each memory which is sticking out a little. This may not mean anything, but in each memory at least one thing is red in color. The reason the color red stands out to me is because of the items that are red. The items are not out of place, but the color does not seem to go with its surroundings. Do you think red can be the way things are labeled in the Time Keeper?" The color 'red' is the only thing Ian can think of, so he wants to find out what Jax thinks.

"Tell me about the items that are red in the memories you were given. You can skip over parts of the memories, but tell me why you think the color of them does not go with the surroundings,"

Jax insists Ian elaborate more on what he is meaning.

"In the four memories I was shown, there was something colored red in each one of them. The first memory was very old. I was able to tell by the room I woke up in which one wall had covered with red wallpaper. The reason the wall stood out to me was because it didn't match the rest of the room walls, which were covered with family paintings, bare stone walls, and hand painted ceilings. The wall with a fireplace large enough to walk into was covered with the red wallpaper covered with some design. The design looked like some type of crest or something. I'm not sure to be exact. Now, the second memory was of an old school classroom and at the head of the room was the teachers' desk which had a single red apple on top of it. The red apple wasn't out of place, it's just that this memory was in black and white except for the apple. The third one was more current, so current the object is the red headphones you are wearing now around your neck right now," Ian looks at Jax with a smirk. "The last memory is not of a time happening yet, but a man at a party is wearing a tuxedo with a red bow tie. For some reason I can tell the original color of the tie is not red, but I'm not sure why," Ian finishes.

"Well, the color red might be a way to recall a memory. You could focus on an item causing that item to become red, which in return becomes a label, would you agree? I'm not sure how finding out the label system will help you find a memory, but figuring out the system help you locate memories easier in the future. Sounds like if you find the red object in a memory, then you found the focal point of the memory. This will not be of any help to you when looking for a specific memory stored by one of you ancestors," Jax tells Ian, "unless you are aware of what the focal point of a memory is that you are looking for."

"I'm not sure. I don't know if I was accessing the memories, or if I was being shown those memories. Is there a possibility of me being led to those memories? Are there any stories of someone being the actual keeper of the Time Keeper, not like me having the watch and access to the memories, but something, or someone bigger, who is responsible for all its contents, or memories?" Ian hints to Jax for more answers.

"Not that I can recall hearing about. Why are you asking?" Jax questions back.

"Well, since I didn't possess any knowledge of how to access the Time Keeper, how should I be able to not only access stored memories but access specific memories? I was never explained to about my family history or the Time Keeper, so what are the odds for me to not only figure out how to access the Time Keeper, but also find select memories of my ancestors to view," Ian replies back to Jax.

"You have a point, but being who you are may be the only thing you need to access the Time Keeper. Maybe the Time Keeper reacts to your bloodline. Your bloodline is one possibility to explain how you accessed the Time Keeper by accident. Now it would not explain how you accessed exact memories, only how you would gain access to the Time Keeper," Jax answers Ian's next question before he can even ask.

"Well, thanks for clearing up my next question, which leaves me with more questions," Ian retorts to Jax.

"Maybe something is in the library at the school that we've not come across yet. We had no reason to think anyone except the current Hele bloodline in possession of the Time Keeper was allowed access the contents, because we had no reason to think any differently. This is the first time any controller of the Time Keeper had accidental access to other memories. All the other Hele bloodline descendants were trained for years, before their eighteenth birthday at the school, on how to gain access and what to expect from its powers and its stored memories. With the Time Keeper being missing for so many years, the training stopped. The school administrators felt without the Time Keeper, teaching any of the next Hele bloodlines would be wasted time. Without the Time Keeper, no Hele bloodline would been in control of the Time Keeper, so no need to train others on how to use the Time Keeper. I bet they are now regretting their decision at this moment," Jax burst out with a short laugh.

"So, is this the reason you are here now? Now that the Time Keeper has been found, and did the school order you to bring me back with you to start my training? This is not a favor for my father, is it?" Ian is questioning Jax for the truth.

"Yes and no. Your father did contact the school once he found the Time Keeper, but he asked them to only send me to meet with you and have you come back with me. So yes, this is a favor for your father. It may not have started out this way, but it is now," Jax expresses to Ian with a little sorrow in his voice.

Ian and Jax make the street exit out of the park, looking as though hailing a cab was going to take a little longer than they expected, Ian thinks it may be a good time to ask a little more about the history of the Time Keeper.

"Jax, while we wait can you tell me more about the history of the Time Keeper?"

Jax looks not only surprised at Ian's request, but also excited and so he begins.

Chapter 12

Helen and Zimmerman

"History tells a tale in which Sebastian Helen and Grayson Zimmerman are such close friends that the bloodlines between their families become destined to find each other throughout the generations to come. They, of course, would not have any knowledge of this destiny of their bloodlines to find each other through past generations, but they always have found each other throughout time. They always become friends in the beginning, best friends one can say, but in the end, they always become enemies with a fight of some kind or another. Destiny was not just uniting their bloodlines, but it was also ending their friendships the same way as Sebastian's and Grayson's ended. History finds a way of repeating itself when these two families' bloodlines are involved. Without the Time Keeper to store any of those moments, becoming friends again was never a possibility," Jax continues on with a little of the Helen and Zimmerman family connection to Ian.

"Remember, when Sebastian and Grayson got into a fight growing up? Back then Sebastian was able to store that moment in the Time Keeper to go back to later. Sebastian always felt that it was something he had done that he could undo to save their friendship, so he would go back and change the stored moment's outcome, thus keeping their friendship alive. His usage became more frequent as they grew older. After their last fight, with Sebastian's inability to find the Time Keeper and store the horrible fight between them in the Time Keeper, he would never be able to go back and change the outcome of that moment in time. From that point on, your bloodlines' destinies have been in a cycle of repeating the same events, becoming friends and then enemies. Without a place for someone from your family bloodline to store those moments which ended their friendships and to go back to change the outcomes, your families became enemies and continued to become enemies."

"Well, if our bloodlines are meant to find each other throughout the generations, we can assume Talbot Wisner is a descendant of Peter Hele, since Talbot was able to access the Time Keeper. In that case, wouldn't that also mean he had a friend who would have become his enemy, someone from the Zimmerman bloodline that destiny would have been connected to him?" Ian suggests to Jax. "Do you think his death could also be connected to his friend? I mean since there were no other stories of the Time Keeper being used, after his death up until two years ago?" Ian extends an alternative ending to Talbot's death to Jax.

"Your way of thinking of this, as an outsider looking in, has given you an advantage and a point of view that could explain a couple of other things as well," Jax reconfirms to Ian. This new approach of looking at Talbot makes Jax question if he's overlooked other things as important as this over the years. Could there be other things he may have missed? Jax starts to think that once the rest of the Believers learn of this information, they may come to the same assumptions and wonder what all they may have overlooked, just as Ian interrupts his wandering mind.

"What do you mean a couple of other things?" Ian cracks back at Jax as he can tell his mind is heading in another direction.

"Well, for starters, this is a new lead that may explain Talbot's death, what happened to the Time Keeper for all those years, and even the possibility of solving the murder of the man from two years ago. We now can assume the murdered man is a relative of yours, and if you remember the man arrested for his murder said someone hired him for the hit. He never did reveal who hired him for the job, but I bet if we dig deeper into the man's murder, we will find a man named Mason was the one who hired the hit-man. Mason will also connect back to the Zimmerman family bloodline," Jax explains to Ian.

"How can you know the name of the man who hired the hit-man and not mention that fact to me earlier?"

"I didn't tell you his name in the first place for a reason. It's not what you may be thinking. I swear I will explain more about Mason later, but for now we need to stay focused on our current discussion, the one of the history of Hele and Zimmerman. You may be able to fill in some more of the blanks in our history section, once we make our way to the school," Jax insists to Ian. "Once we arrive at the school, we can then access the school's library."

"Why don't we go to the school library now?" Ian questions Jax.

"The school's library is not as simple to get to as it may sound, Ian. You see, the school is not actually here in New York City, or even the State of New York. The school I teach at, and the one you will be attending again, is in Texas," Jax tells Ian. "The first time you attended the school though, before history changed, we didn't look into these types of questions, because you did not learn any of this information until now."

"What direction are you talking about? What blanks do you think I can fill in? We are guessing, because we are nowhere closer to filling in any blanks than we were a few minutes ago. I'm still just as clueless now as I was a few minutes ago, about everything," Ian sounds upset. "There is one thing..."

"What is that one thing Ian?" Jax inquires.

"Well, since you said our bloodlines' connection repeats throughout history, what's the possibility of those two children fighting in the old school classroom memory being connected? Remember the two children outside the old school classroom fighting that I overheard before I knocked over the globe, heavy enough to make all the noise that I think they actually heard? I told you they stopped fighting and started asking if someone was in the room. Now, what's important here is the fact I heard two boys fighting in one of the memories," Ian tries to jog Jax memory.

"I'm sorry Ian. You're correct, you may think your knowledge about your history and the Time Keeper is small, but as you can see now, you have become a tremendous deal of help to us. The questions you ask and the assumptions you come up with can explain a lot about the history gaps we have had at the school regarding the Time Keeper. You are able to give us some great leads and places to start looking for answers we never had before.

Now, what else can you think of, either from what you learned from me or what you learned on your own, something that may not have made sense to you then or now?" Jax requests of Ian with excitement.

"Well, to be honest with you, I think I have to be more up front with you about the last dream, or memory as you call it," Ian confesses to Jax.

"Like what?"

"You remember when I, let's say, gained access to select memories, correct?" Ian reminds Jax.

"Yes, I remember, of course. Now, go on," Jax instructs Ian.

"Okay, remember the first two of the memories shown to me were of the past and the third one was more current," Ian reveals to Jax. "You know, the one of us meeting in the park and you wearing the red headphones around your neck?"

"Yes, I remember you telling me about those, but you also mentioned a fourth memory. A memory of a man at a party wearing the red bow tie," Jax recalls to Ian.

"Yes, the last memory shown to me, but I cannot say if it was in the past or the present. I don't want to say it was of the future either, because if it is, then I'm accessing future memories. That alone means we are either not current or someone else is in control of the Time Keeper. Also, if it was of the future, what about if the outcome has changed? You know, since Kayla is no longer part of this history, the memory may not become an event at all." Ian is trying to avoid telling Jax the last memory, since he is in the last one.

"What are you not telling me? You are holding something back from me and I want to know what that is. I'm not sure about where you are going with the future part yet, or someone else controlling the Time Keeper, but it is worth looking into. So, yes, to answer your question, the future is not set in stone, and anyone's future can change depending on what choices they make in life. Humor me and tell me about the last memory you saw," Jax pleads with Ian.

"Okay, well the last memory shown to me is of a party of some sort. The party is being held in the penthouse of a tall building in New York City. I don't remember seeing anyone young at the party except myself, but as I think more about the party, I'm not sure exactly how old I am. The memory does not last very long, but I do remember seeing one person at the party that I did recognized," Ian pauses for a moment.

"Go on, who's this person?" Jax hopes Ian finishes.

"You. You are the other person I recognize at the party Jax, it's you. You are the one all dressed up in a tuxedo. You are the man in the red bow tie. In the memory, as I am making my way over to speak to you, I look down to check the time, but I find the Time Keeper is missing. Then the next thing I know, I get awakened by Kayla. She had come over early yesterday, after my eighteenth birthday surprise party, and was knocking on my bedroom door. She's the reason I woke up," Ian finishes repeating the details of his fourth and final dream to Jax. "So now you see why I'm asking if someone else possess the ability to control the Time Keeper. The last memory is not one from me, or at least not yet. If it is my memory, then how many times have I repeated being seventeen? What if this is a memory, but it is not mine? Since I can access all the memories placed in the Time Keeper, what are the possibilities of me accessing a memory that will be stored in the Time Keeper later by one of my future relatives?"

Jax looked surprised at Ian's last remark about the number of times one may be seventeen and the possibility of a future relative storing a memory which he accessed. Jax is not sure how to answer either of these questions. Well, before today, Jax would have told Ian he is only seventeen once, but this is Ian's second seventeenth birthday. Before today, Jax never would have thought about the possibility for anyone to access future memories in the Time Keeper. Before today, he also thought only the one who stored a memory in the Time Keeper possessed the abilities in accessing it. After the day Jax and Ian have had, Jax came up with several questions of his own for the Council. Questions he will only be able to ask once they make their way to the school. The Council must be holding something back from me about the history of the Time Keeper, or there is something else they are leaving out. Jax is familiar with the Council's practice of leaving information out. Jax will find out what they know about the Time Keeper, one way or another, when they arrive at the school.

"Ian, I can't answer those questions at this time. I'm sorry, but this is all new to me as well. To my knowledge, this is the first time history's been changed in a way in which a keeper's been taken back to the past and left. We are dealing with something new here. I promise you though, we will get to the bottom of this once we are at the school." Jax feels the urge to comfort Ian.

Jax finishes with the history lesson of Hele and Zimmerman just as Ian has flagged down a cab. Jax opens the back door of the cab for Ian to climb into and Jax follows.

"Where to?" questions the cabbie.

"Brooklyn," Ian replies. Ian thinks he's told more cabbies that in the past few days than he has in his lifetime. Although he hates riding in cabs, he let those thoughts pass. Ian is ready to get home and find some answers.

Robert Starnes

Chapter 13

Back to Brooklyn

Jax and Ian sit in the back of the taxi as it heads towards Brooklyn, and Ian wants to see if he can get a few more questions answered before they make it to his apartment.

"Jax, where were my parents when I came out of my room? You remember, on my first seventeenth birthday, when they intended for us to meet?"

"You mean that day I found you in the park on that park bench? Well, remember, I told you that Grayson's descendants also may have knowledge about someone accessing the time lost in the Time Keeper and changing history? Well, not only are they aware of that, but they are also aware that your parents bought the watch a few days before your birthday," Jax begins to answer Ian's question.

"How can that be possible? How would they know about my parents buying the watch, which also just happens to be the actual Time Keeper?"

"Two years ago, after your relative was murdered, the man with the watch, and the police secured the watch as evidence, we, the Believers, found out one of our own, Mason Carpenter, was a descendant of Grayson. Once he became aware of where the Time Keeper was, he felt he had no reason to hide his true identity from us any longer. After he left our group, he started looking for the Time Keeper. He paid off a police officer to retrieve the watch from police evidence to give to him. The police officer does what he is paid to do, and once Mason has possession of the Time Keeper, he heads home.

After Mason is safe and secure at home, he reaches into his pocket to retrieve the watch and then realizes his pocket is empty. He feels that all the trouble he has gone through to get the Time Keeper was for nothing. The Time Keeper is missing again, and Mason cannot think of how he lost such a small object on his way home. He only had possession of the watch for a short time. Mason begins to recall every place he passed on his way home. He thinks of every person's face he crossed paths with on his way home, and then he remembers bumping into a young man. Mason did not think that the innocent looking young man could have been anything more than just a classic case of not watching where he was going. That was until he realized the watch had gone missing upon his arrival home.

The young man who casually bumped into Mason pick pocketed the watch from him, ever so slightly. The sly thief, unknowing of the watch's history or power, knew he needed to get rid of the watch as soon as possible. He made this his first priority. Since his friend worked at an old book store, the book store where your parents bought the Time Keeper, he set up a meeting with the owner and sold the watch to him. The owner gave a great deal for the watch, but little would he realize the watch would sit in the glass cabinet, never to be sold, at least until your parents stopped in to purchase it. The Time Keeper sat in the glass cabinet for two years, and Mason never gave up on looking for it either.

Mason spent the next two years looking for that young man who picked his pockets and stole the Time Keeper from him. He figured if he wanted to find the watch again, first he needed to find the thief. Mason hired a private detective to help with his search. They both searched pawn shops all over the city, but they came up with nothing at every shop. No one at any of the pawn shops that they spoke to about the thief, had any information about the young man described. They knew nothing of the watch in the photos he showed either. A few days before your parents bought the Time Keeper, Mason heard pawn shops aren't the only places to look for unique items. With his new found information, he extended his search criteria to include antique stores, second hand shops, and bookstores. It was not long after he expanded his search area, Mason hit his payday.

Mason started receiving more information than he expected and could ever process about antique watches. By the time he was able to sort out what were to be considered good leads, his time had run out. Your parents had already purchased the Time Keeper. Mason followed up on the leads to see which ones could led him to the Time Keeper. Once one of those leads turned out to be the one that had taken him to the book store your parents bought the watch from, and he found out it was already sold. He did what he had to do to the store owner to find out who had purchased the watch. He was not afraid to use tough methods of questioning someone, in order to get information about anything, which he used on the store owner to find out who he sold the watch to. While the store owner was unable to give him your parents' actual names, he was able to give him the only information he could remember about the sale and that was how they paid for it.

Mason is so desperate for the watch that he stole the store owner's sales receipts and records for the past few months. That is how he found out where you and your parents live. Afraid of being found by us, the Believers, he hired some guys to retrieve the watch back from your parents by any means necessary. The men he hired went to your apartment. At first sight of your father wearing a watch, they assumed the watch must be the one they were hired to get back, so they kidnapped your parents and took them to that traitor, Mason. Once he saw your father was wearing the wrong watch, he let your parents go. By the time they arrived home, you had already gone searching for them and ended up at the park with me. I made a split decision, to be on the safe side, to take you straight to the school," Jax tells Ian. Jax can tell that Ian is feeling relief knowing his parents are safe.

"So, while we were traveling to the school, my parents, to your knowledge, were safe?" Ian wants more details.

"Yes, and so did you. But you don't remember any of this, do you?"

"No, and since you're bringing up the subject, why can't I remember anything about being at the school, or anything from the year I was eighteen?"

"To be honest Ian, I'm not sure. History says the one who can access the memories, can also change history and can still remember the original history timeline before any changes were made. Something powerful must have happened to you before you came back, repeating your seventeenth birthday, to cause you to forget the past year as though you never were eighteen. This is something I have never heard about or ever come across before. You say when you arrived home, the last time you left the park your parents gave you a surprise eighteenth birthday party?"

"Yes, that's correct. It's like they were expecting me. Like I was coming home after being gone for some time, but I don't recall where I had been. Now, I do know that they were expecting me," Ian answers Jax.

"How can you be certain that they were expecting you?" Jax expresses wonder to Ian.

"Well, they were throwing me a surprise birthday party," Ian replies with a smirk. "Hey, how do you remember details of this past year and of me being at your school? Do you think my parents will remember as well? How is it that I cannot remember?"

"We, Believers, are affected by the changes of events in history, in some ways or others, yet we still remember history before the changes. We don't understand how, or why, you were able to access the moments and delete a whole year of your history," Jax stops. "Did anything happen at your eighteenth birthday party that might seem to be out of the ordinary or unusual?"

"Well, the only thing which comes to mind is something about my friend Kayla, the one that no one remembers now. She was acting a little different," Ian recalls.

"What do you mean different?"

"Well, for starters, we have never exchanged gifts for our birthdays before, but that year she gave me a gift. This ring I'm wearing is the gift she gave me. This is the same ring I put on with the watch on my eighteenth birthday we talked about earlier," Ian tells Jax, while pointing at his right hand ring finger. "The ring only fits over the first knuckle, but something strange is written inside. I asked her what the writing said, but she replied she had no clue, and that she bought the ring at some old store. When I put the ring on for the first time, I swear I felt it vibrate. There was also something in the strange way that she spoke about the ring and writing inside of it. I got the sense she might have been holding something back. So later, I told her about my dreams. After I told her about my dreams I started asking her more about the ring, but she became defensive and avoided my questions. As she was walking out of my room, the last words I heard her speak were, 'It's just a ring Ian. You can wear the ring or not, but I hope you do,' which I thought was a bit odd. Once she had left, I decided I needed to get up, so I removed the ring and placed it next to the watch on my dresser. I gathered my things for a shower, and headed to the bathroom. Once I finished my shower, brushed my teeth, and brushed my hair, I headed back to my room to get dressed. I got dressed for the day and all I had left to do was to put on my watch and ring, which I did, and that is when IT happened."

"What do you mean by, 'IT' happened?"

"Well, when I put on the ring Kayla gave me, in an instant, a flash of memories started rushing through my mind, except they were not going in a normal order. You see, they were flashing in reverse. They hit me so hard and fast I had to grab ahold of my dresser just to keep from being thrown backwards. The rush of the reverse memories felt like it was happening for a long time, but I know it happened quickly, because as fast and hard as it started, it stopped," Ian finishes.

"Okay, now that is something you should have led with. That sounds like some sort of a history wipe, and you say that it happened when you put on the ring that Kayla gave you?" Jax speculates as he points at Kayla's ring on Ian's finger.

"Yes, but how could Kayla be involved with any of this? She doesn't live in the same apartment as she did before. So, she doesn't even exist in this time line now. Why would she be involved with a history wipe that would not only erase a year of my life but also erase her from time? And if she did do this, how can I remember her?" Ian questions Jax's motive. "Back to another subject real quick if you don't mind. If I am the only one who can access this thing, why does Mason want the Time Keeper?" Ian shoots Jax one more question.

"His true intentions are unknown at this time, but we think he wants to go back to the beginning when the Time Keeper is invented by Peter Hele. We believe he is going to try and force you into accessing the first time lost," Jax pauses for a moment, as he is debating whether or not to tell Ian the rest of the theory.

"Well, go on," Ian wants to hear more.

"To be blunt, you and your parents are not safe here in the city. Mason will stop at nothing until he can find a way to make you go back and take the Time Keeper from Peter Hele and give the watch to one of his ancestors. He believes Peter possesses the ability to transfer the power to access the Time Keeper to another person, and he wants the power to be transferred to his family bloodline. Remember, Sebastian is the one who told Grayson about the Hele family legacy regarding the Time Keeper in the first place. Those two thought of themselves as real brothers. Sebastian thought if something happened to him, he wanted Grayson to carry on the family legacy of the Time Keeper. Little did he know it was impossible for Grayson to carry on his family legacy, as the Time Keeper's access was created for, and only achievable, within the Hele bloodline not, Grayson's bloodline. The word around our people, the Believers, is Mason wants to go back and change his family history and yours too."

"After Sebastian and Grayson parted ways, without Sebastian being able to go back and resolve their dispute, history says Grayson became an unhappy person. He became drunker than usual and became an abusive man to his children, who in turn, passed down the same behavior for many generations to come. Grayson, during his drunken stupors, and while beating his children, would ramble on about Sebastian's family magic watch and how he could go back in time. He would continue this type of behavior so often his young boys would grow up doing and saying the exact same things to their children.

You may have figured out by now, Mason Carpenter is a descendant of Grayson Zimmerman. He, himself, is unable to produce children of his own, due to injuries he received from years of abuse by his own father. Mason thinks you can use the Time Keeper to access one of Peter Hele's first memories, and transfer the power of the Time Keeper over to his family's bloodline, therefore never having to grow up with the abuse he endured as a child. What Mason does not understand is going back in history to change anything could result in disastrous results. Not only can they end with his birth never happening, but there is no telling what the real ending can hold. Who is to say what changes can happen by one small alteration in time by the wrong person? The possible changes are endless."

"Whoa, that IS awful!" Ian exclaims.

"You're right, that really is awful, and there are other ways to break cycles of family abuse. To Mason, this is his last chance since he will be the last descendant of Grayson Zimmerman. The saddest part, to me, is his revenge is fueled by Sebastian trusting Grayson so much he wholeheartedly thought, since they considered themselves brothers, they would both be able to use the Time Keeper. The story's been told so many times, down through so many generations of the Zimmerman bloodlines, as a magical watch by so many of the abusive, drunken Zimmerman fathers, Mason will never believe the truth now. The powers of the Time Keeper could never be, then or now, transferred to anyone. The Time

Keeper is, and forever will be, linked to the Hele family bloodline since he is its creator."

Jax is finishing as they are pulling up in front of Ian's apartment building. Ian has finished asking Jax questions. He is ready to get his seventeenth birthday, for the second time, over with.

The taxi stops and Ian quickly climbs out of the backseat for the sidewalk. He starts walking towards the building entrance and stops. Ian does not know what to expect this time when he goes inside his apartment. *Is there going to be a surprise party for me, is my mom going to be worried, since I left in a hurry this morning with little word on when I would be back, or will my parents even be home? How can you prepare for something, when you know change is possible at any moment, even if it's by accident?* Ian was walking into his apartment building left with even more questions.

Robert Starnes

Chapter 14

The Beginning of Home

"Wait Ian, I have some things that I must tell you before you see your parents," Jax shouts as he is paying the driver. He can tell by the way Ian is not stopping that Ian is in no mood to listen to any of what Jax has to say.

Ian just keeps walking towards the apartment entrance without even a glance back to Jax, or any acknowledgement of even hearing him, and vanishes through the front doors out of Jaxs sight.

Ian starts his way up to the third floor using the stairs, of course, as the elevator has not worked in years. As he passes what used to be Kayla's floor, he had the urge to try her door one last time, but he didn't. He continues up the stairs until he reaches his floor, steps out of the stairwell, and walks down the hall to his door, just as Jax is making his way out of the stairwell. Jax was too late. Ian was walking into his apartment before Jax could stop him.

"Mom, Dad, sorry I'm so late. I lost track of time today," Ian rambles. "I hope I did not cause you to worry too much."

"Where were you all day? We've been very concerned about you, ever since you left in such a hurry this morning and did not say when you would be returning. I had to call your father and ask him if he had seen you," expresses Ian's mother.

"We are very happy you are safe. Now, we've got some things to tell you. You may want to take a seat before we start," added Ian's father.

Ian takes a seat on the couch, and before either of his parents can speak, Ian speaks first. "Well, before we dive into all the things you need to tell me, I need to tell you something too." Before Ian can finish, Jax enters the apartment. "I think you may know Jax, and now so do I. Jax and I spent the last few hours together and have spoken, in great detail, about a few things. I have some idea what you are about to speak to me about, maybe some of the same things, so we may be able to save some time. Trust me, I still have a ton of questions for you. Now I think Jax may have few questions of his own. Don't get me wrong, I'm glad to be home. I am very happy the both of you are here, but for now, I will sit here and let the three of you talk," Ian suggests to his parents and Jax.

Ian was relieved, as the three were left smiling, after the hint of shock and surprise overcame his parents' faces.

"Jax, how did you find Ian? Why didn't you come to the apartment like we planned? How in the world did this introduction become so messed up?" Ian's father asks with concern. "Don't misunderstand me, Jax. We are grateful you found him and that you are both safe but has something changed that we are not aware of?"

"Well, a few changes have occurred," Jax replies.

"How come we cannot sense any changes in history or remember anything different? What is going on here Jax?" Ian's father questions Jax with demand.

"Well, I am not sure to be honest. Some new developments we've never come across before, or heard of before, came up today. I don't want the two of you to worry about that right now. Until more information is available, let's keep our focus on the original plan. Okay? So until I can make sure Ian arrives at school, I won't be able to find out many of the answers to your questions. Please trust me for now. I can tell you that some of the changes which happened were positive changes for you, but don't ask me anything about them during this time," Jax stops.

"Okay, well, how did you end up with Ian in the first place? You are not supposed to meet him until tonight, here at his birthday party, or are these parts of the changes we are not to speak about?" Ian's mother questions Jax.

"I found Ian in Central Park near Belvedere Castle, and he was looking for you," Jax explains. "And yes, this will be an area of those changes we will not discuss at this time. What I can tell you is that Ian was able to access the Time Keeper and change some things, recent things. Now he did not do this on his own. Someone appears to have helped him because they needed him to delete, not only a year of his life and a year of everyone else's life, but also erase their own existence completely from history. This was done by giving him something else that when it is put close to the Time Keeper works with it. When this item was placed near the Time Keeper, Ian gained access to the Time Keeper and the item did a history wipe on him. Again, I am only speculating at this. I cannot find any real proof until we get to the school. For now this is all I can say," Jax terminates the conversation.

"That still does not explain why Ian went to Belvedere Castle, Jax. Are you avoiding answering a certain part of this question?" Ian's mother spits venom in her tone.

"Yes I am but for a very good reason. Before the change in history when Ian came out of his room on his seventeenth birthday, you two had been kidnapped. Ian went out looking for you but found me instead. Does that answer your question? I told you there are positive changes involving you, and this is one of them," Jax answers her question with a stern expression on his face to stop her from asking any more questions.

"What do you mean seventeenth birthday? That is today. There has to be more to this story than you are telling us Jax." Ian's father's not pleased about being left in the dark.

"That is correct. I told you that there are some changes we will not be able to talk about at this time," Jax replies to Ian's father.

"Well, how could it be possible for him to access the Time Keeper anyway? He is not even of age yet. Ian will not be able to access the Time Keeper until he is eighteen. How does he now possess the Time Keeper anyway? We've been looking for the Time Keeper for years and have had no luck in finding it. How can he be wearing the watch now?"

"I noticed the watch on Ian's wrist this morning. When I asked him about it, he told me he found the watch in the back of a cab last night. Ian's mother elaborates a little more. Is the watch he's wearing the actual Time Keeper?"

"Yes, it's the real thing. That is the true Time Keeper. I can tell you he did not come in possession of the Time Keeper by accident, but that you found the watch in an old bookstore. You purchased the Time Keeper and gave it to Ian for his first seventeenth birthday, but this is also a part of history that has now been changed, so now it has never happened. Before you ask, no, we don't understand how Ian's wearing the watch now, but he is. Let's just say he was of age, for a very short time, until today," Jax ends this line of questioning.

Both of Ian's parents glance over at him with shame in their eyes and an expression of guilt for everything that has been happening to him. Ian begins to say something to his parents, but Jax stops him abruptly. Ian wants his parents to understand that he does not blame them for any of this. He is not mad at them. He is just glad they are home and safe.

"I need to speak to Ian for a few minutes alone if you don't mind," Jax respectfully request of Ian's parents. Ian's parents set off to the kitchen to give Jax and Ian some privacy. Ian watches them stroll off to the kitchen, still with the same look of shame and guilt on their faces. Ian wishes there was something he could do to assure them that he loves them, and he believes everything will be fine.

"Now, before you start telling your parents about today, keep in mind, to them, today is their first time having today. Remember, when your memories and your history was deleted for the past year, everyone's future events were wiped as well, for the time being. Your father is of your bloodline, and your mother is a Believer, but for some reason, they don't remember you being at school for a year, just like you don't remember being there. You cannot tell them too much about what we talked about or what you may remember. This could end up being too much for time to be able to heal, since will catch up after a year of being deleted from your life. We may tell them too much, so we need to be careful of what we say. So to be on the safe side, let's not over load them, agreed?" Jax waits for an agreement from Ian, but instead receives a nod from Ian as a sign of understanding, just as his parents were coming back into the room.

Ian is back at home, his exhaustion has caught up with him, and he is so confused about everything he's learned today. He cannot remember when the last time he had a good night's rest was. To Ian, whenever he went to sleep, he either experienced someone else's memories, ended up losing a year of his life, or worse. He is the only person that can remember Kayla's life, which to him is worse than forgetting her existence. His parents are in safe hands since Jax is here.

"Why don't you try and get some rest before you fall over on the couch," as if Ian's mother can read the blank stare on his face. This is the best suggestion Ian's heard all day, even as much as it scares him to sleep because of the dreams, he still needs rest.

Ian stands up and turns to walk out of the living room towards his bedroom, and he turns his head at his parents hoping they will understand he does not blame them for any of this. Ian's parents and Jax return to their seats, and Jax figures he needs to tell them a few of the things that changed with their history. He is smart enough to understand why he may not be able to tell them too much, and not to reveal information about Kayla's part in this or the powers of the ring she gave Ian, but he needs to ask them about her.

Once Ian leaves for his room to get some rest, Jax fills Ian's parents in on what he told Ian about his family history and the Time Keeper and about what they avoided by the deleting the past year of their lives. Jax explains Ian's friend Kayla to his parents, but as he is speaking about her, they both stare at him with blank expressions on their faces. They do not recall who she is, or who he is talking about. After Jax fills them in on everything Ian confirmed, except for the ring Kayla gave him, Jax is confident the ring Kayla gave Ian must be something powerful and dark. Jax does not tell them Kayla is more involved with these events, even though she deleted herself from history, from everyone except Ian. Kayla wants, or needs, Ian to remember her. Why is the real question? Jax does not want them to worry about Kayla using Ian as she did once before and could possibly try to again.

Ian still has some questions, but as tired as he is they can wait. The sooner Ian gets to his bedroom, the sooner he can change clothes and crawl into his bed and sleep. His mind and body are so heavy like they worked overtime all day. Ian takes a seat on his bed, takes off his boots, and before he can change out of his street clothes, he has already fallen back on his bed and is fast asleep.

Ian drifts off to sleep, but he cannot help but worry. He worries about Kayla and where she is now. He worries about the ring she gave him, what she has to do with this, and worried about the watch and its powers. He cannot stop wondering how he can be wearing a watch never given to him since history has changed. *Could history change because of the powers of the ring and watch together? Did Kayla give me the ring with the knowledge of its power? Did she know that the powers of the watch and ring together would delete a year of everyone's life? Did she know it would delete her from history completely?* Ian couldn't finish another thought before he was in a deep sleep.

***

"Now I will try to answer your question about your special bond with Ian, or connection. You see, when you both are eighteen your ability to communicate with each other through your dreams became active. Now Ian is not aware of this nor is anyone else. You and I are the only ones in this timeline aware of this about the two of you. Neither the Council, nor the Believers, are aware of it, and we have to keep it this way for as long as we can. I cannot tell you why the two of you have this connection, not yet, but I'm glad you asked."

"Are you going to teach me how to use this connection? Can I tell Ian, so he can contact me as well?" Kayla is shooting back more questions with excitement.

"You said one question, and I answered it. That is all I can answer for now. We will go over everything else later, but for now you need to rest. The next part is going to be a lot for you to take in, and you will need your strength. Trust me."

"Very well, I trust you, like I said before." Then she shut her eyes, and she drifted off to sleep.

While Kayla is asleep, Alexis makes a phone call to discuss some type of arrangements she has made for Kayla's protection. After the conversation is over, Alexis sits back in the chair she has been occupying to take a moment to rest herself.

Alexis must have needed more rest than she thought, because she came to with a sudden shock of awareness and saw Kayla sitting up in the bed just staring at her. "How long have I been asleep, and how long have you been watching me?"

"About thirty minutes, except I will not say I was watching you sleep, because you are still blurry to me. Now I am able to sit up and move though," replies Kayla with a giggle. "I bet I freaked you out when you woke up to me sitting here facing you."

"I'm not freaked out. I was caught off guard," Alexis smirks back. "I was not expecting to fall asleep in the first place much less waking up to you looking at me."

"Well, I may not be able to see, but I can tell you that I am hungry. You have anything to eat around here?"

"Sure, let me grab you the fried chicken and mashed potatoes that you are craving. That is what you want isn't it?"

"How do you ...," Kayla doesn't finish her sentence. Kayla thinks since Alexis is from the future, there's no need to ask any questions, because Alexis should also know the answers to any questions even before she can ask them. "Well, since you are from the future, this should make things easy for me. I won't need to tell you when I am hungry or what I want to eat. So breakfast, lunch and dinner should never be late and will be exactly what I want to eat. This is perfect actually, because you will also be able to pause during the story so I won't have to tell you when I need to use the restroom, and I won't interrupt you," Kayla's having a good time with all the new information she's received.

Alexis is beside Kayla's bed with the plate of fried chicken and mashed potatoes for her to eat. She sets the plate down on the bed in front of Kayla, then grabs her hands and moves one over to the silverware for the potatoes and the other one to a chicken leg. These are the only instructions Kayla needs.

Kayla picks up the chicken leg so fast and starts moving it towards her face. Alexis thought she was going to miss her mouth and poke her eye out. To her surprise, Kayla hit her mouth right on the mark. She was not kidding when she said she was hungry, because she will continue to eat until every last bit of chicken and potatoes is gone.

Alexis takes advantage of Kayla eating, while her mouth is full, and begins to continue telling Kayla the things she needs to know to make sure she is prepared for what is going to come next. "While you eat I will continue to tell you a few more things you are going to need to know. Since we don't have as much time left together as I would like, please just listen up and let me finish. After you finish eating, I am going to have to put you in a deep sleep. That is the only way for me to give you some memories you will need. Some of these memories will be real, while others will be fake. The fake ones are only there to help you survive until we figure out how to bring you back safely. You will not understand them at first, but you will when you wake up. I am asking you to put a lot more trust in me, but I will never lie to you or put you in danger. I am telling you the truth and you can tell deep down inside that I am," Alexis completes prepping Kayla.

Kayla is still eating, so she nods her head with an "Okay."

"You will be able to tell which ones are for you and which ones are for your survival. Now, to answer one of your previous questions, no, you will not be able to tell Ian anything about me or any of the things I told you or about your connection. You will not be able to tell him about the memories you are about to receive either. It is very important you understand this, no matter how much you will want to tell him, you cannot ever tell Ian or anyone else. Do you understand?" Alexis demands of Kayla.

By the time when Alexis asks, Kayla has finished eating and is able to answer her back, "Yes, I understand."

"Okay, I hope you are ready, because we are just about out of time. Now, lie back on the bed and close your eyes. It is time for me to put you into a deep sleep for now, so I can transfer those memories to your mind that you are going to need. Now, when you wake up, you will be aware of where you are and who you are with, along with many other memories, but when you first wake up you will be hit with all the memories at once. So your first thought will be of you having a headache, and you will want to take a hot bath. That will give you the time you need to let all the memories settle in your mind, so you can prepare for what you need to do when you finish your bath. Are you ready?"

This is Kayla's only chance to back out, but that would be, if she had a choice.

"Yes, I'm ready," Kayla replies as she closes her eyes.

Alexis is aware this will not take long to complete the memories transfer, and she is done in a flash. Now that the memories are in Kayla's mind, Alexis picks up the phone and makes a call.

"She is all yours. Are you ready to come and pick her up?" Alexis says to the person on the other end of the phone. "Fine, come over and pick her up but don't forget our deal. You remember what I can, and will, do to you if you fail me. You remember, don't you Mason?" Alexis makes her promises to Mason, then hangs up the phone.

Alexis bends down and gives Kayla a kiss on her forehead, turns around and leaves her there on the bed, alone in the apartment. Alexis walks out of the apartment closing the unlocked door behind her, since Mason will be there in a few minutes. She leaves knowing she is doing the right thing.

Kayla is in the deep sleep Alexis put her in to receive the memories she needed. She is starting to understand some of them, but she wants to put those aside for the moment and try to reach out to Ian. She is not sure if she will be able to, but she at least has to try. "Ian! Can you hear me? It's me, Kayla," she speaks with her mind. "Can you hear me?"

***

"Yes I can hear you. Why are you doing this to me? What did I ever do to you to make you want to delete yourself from my past, my life, and history itself?" Ian replies to her voice. Ian cannot see a face or anything of her, although he can hear the sound of HER voice in his mind.

"I never wanted you to forget me, and you haven't have you? No, you haven't! That is why I told you to wear the ring. I am so sorry Ian. I never wanted to be a part of any of this, but I had no choice in this, just like you didn't. Our lives were destined to cross paths from the time we were born, but there is one thing Mason Carpenter does not, and cannot, ever find out about us. Please don't ask me what it is, because the less you know the safer you are. That is why I did what I did. That is why the ring not only wiped me from history, but also sent you back to your seventeenth birthday. That was so you now have been given a head start to prepare for what is to come. You see, you contain more information now than you did during your first year at your school, which is what you are going to need if you plan on restoring me back into history. I must go before I wake up, but please don't let anyone take that ring away from you. I am sorry Ian, but I need to go and this is goodbye." Then Kayla's voice is gone.

Ian opens his eyes for a moment and a wet tear runs down the side of his face. The pain he is experiencing is not his, but Kayla's. After the pain passes, Ian closes his eyes and goes back to sleep. This time, no dreams, no voices, no interruptions will wake him until morning comes.

***

Kayla's head is beginning to hurt, and she recalls what she was told to do when she wakes up.

Chapter 15

Kayla Meets Mason

Kayla loses her connection with Ian and begins to gain conciseness. Her head starts pounding just as Alexis said it would. As she starts coming to, the only thing she can think of is that she wants to take a hot bath.

Kayla opens her eyes, sits up in bed and tells the nurse, who is sitting in the chair beside the bed, that she wants to speak to Mason. The nurse jumps up without a pause and takes off out of the room. Kayla assumes the nurse is going to bring Mason up to speed, that she is awake and asking to speak to him. She is still not sure who Mason is, but she does know he is who she is supposed to ask for because her new memories tell her that he is the one in charge. The nurse does not take long to return with the man Kayla recognizes immediately as Mason.

"It's good to see that you are awake. How are you feeling today?" Mason takes notice of Kayla's expression.

"To be honest with you, my head is killing me. Do you mind if I take a hot bath? A hot bath always helps me with my headaches," Kayla replies.

"Yes, of course you may. Nurse, please take Kayla down to the bathing room and leave her, so she may take as much time as she needs," Mason orders the nurse. "Buzz the intercom from the bathing room when you are ready, and I will send the nurse back to retrieve you. With everything that you have been through, we don't want you falling down and hurting yourself after just waking up. You need to rest and gather your strength back. Having a clear head is a great place to start," Mason finishes.

Mason leaves the room as the nurse walks over to the bed and helps Kayla from the bed to the wheelchair. Once she is all settled in the chair, the nurse begins to wheel her out of her room and down the hall. From what Kayla can gather from the jumbled memories she received from Alexis and what she can see with her own eyes, she is not in a hospital. Kayla, knowing she is not in a hospital is set a little at ease, but not too much considering her head is still pounding. The nurse stops only two doors down from Kayla's original room, opens the door and wheels her in. To Kayla's surprise, the bathroom is spacious with a large garden tub. The nurse makes sure there is nothing more Kayla needs from her, then turns and walks out of the bathroom closing the door behind her. Once the door is closed, Kayla begins to climb out of the wheelchair and stand for the first time. She walks over and locks the bathroom door. Now that the door is locked, she turns around and makes her way back over to the inviting garden tub.

As she sits on the edge of the garden tub, Kayla reaches over and turns the faucet on leaving the water to rush out. With the water running, she is able to check the temperature to make sure it not too hot for her but warm enough for her to be able to relax in until her head stops hurting. Kayla finds the perfect temperature, puts the drain stopper in place at the bottom of the tub, and lets the water start to fill the garden size tub. While the tub is filling with warm water, Kayla begins undressing which is not hard for her even in her condition, since she is ready to get in the water so her head will stop hurting. She removes her last piece of clothing, throws her legs over the edge of the tub and dips her feet into the warm water.

Kayla is not prepared for what comes next. She realizes, that when her history wiped, some of her senses wiped as well. She can tell what water is, but she is unable to remember the sensation of water washing over her feet. So she is able to experience that sensation for the first time, again. Even the water's temperature is sending mixed signals through Kayla's body. The sensation is so intense that she begins to ease the rest of her body down into the tub. She is letting the water rush over her bare legs and thighs while taking in this new sensation of warm water. She is no longer paying attention to her head hurting. Kayla is just sitting in the tub letting it fill with water with no other worries on her mind. The more the tub fills with the warm water, and the more of her body the water touches, the more sensational her body becomes. *This must be why Alexis wanted me to take a hot bath while the memories settled. She must have known the history wipe would remove my memory of the sensation of water rushing against my body. That way, as I'm sitting in this warm tub of water, this new sensation has taken my mind off the pain. Alexis did think of everything,* Kayla thinks with only a little pain.

She continues to concentrate on this new sensation of warm water, so her new memories are able to fill her mind and settle in with ease. The memories begin to settle, and she begins to relax and enjoy the warm water. In doing so, she forgets to turn the water off, and the water was almost at the top of the tub before she noticed. She reaches up and turns the faucet off as quickly as she can. Now that the water is off, she rests back into the water and begins to recall some of the memories she's been given. She remembers that some of them are real and some are fake. The fake ones were given to her for her survival. She will need time to sort them out but at least she's got all the time she needs while in the bathroom. Now that she is aware of why she is with Mason, for her protection, she still does not know why she needs to be with him. She does not understand how he is going to be able to protect her. The only people she can trust are Alexis and Ian, even though she has been instructed not to contact Ian. But since she has contacted him once before, she comes to the conclusion she is going to have to try again. This is not the time though. She is going to take this time to finish relaxing and letting the warm water steam up the room until her head does not hurt at all.

Kayla is not sure how long she has been taking her hot bath, but once her head stops throbbing, she pulls the stopper from the bottom of the tub so the water can drain. The tub begins the empty as she climbs out and starts to dry off the best she can. The hot bath not only helped with her being able to relax and accept the memory rush, but it also relaxed her muscles as well. She was not prepared for the limited mobility of her arms. Now that her head's not pounding, like when she first entered the bathroom, she notices that there is a fresh set of clothes for her to put on. She does not care how they got there, or whose idea the clothes were, she is just glad they are there. Once she finishes dressing, and has a clearer mind, she presses the button on the intercom as instructed.

"Are you all finished with your bath?" replies the voice through the speaker.

"Yes, I'm ready to go back to my room, if that's not going to be a problem." There's no reply, but a few minutes later there is a knock on the door. Kayla had forgotten she had locked the door after the nurse had left. She makes her way over and unlocks the door, but before she can return to the wheelchair, she is grabbed from behind by the nurse. Kayla is unable to react to her in a threatening way before the nurse begins to help her into the wheelchair. Between being wiped from history and being given all these new memories, the last thing she needs to worry about is if the nurse is going to hurt her.

They make their way from the bathroom back to her room, as Kayla is starting to piece together some of the memories she was given. She is beginning to understand why she is with Mason and how he is going to protect her, though she does understand the true purpose. Kayla can predict what Mason could do with the information, if he were to find out about the connection she shares with Ian, things would become bad for the both of them. She now understands why Mason can never find out about their special connection. They arrive back at her room, the nurse pushes open the door and wheels Kayla in, where Mason just happens to be waiting.

"I hope you don't mind that I am in here, but there are a few things I want to speak to you about before you eat and rest," Mason is speaking to Kayla as if the nurse is not in the room with them.

"No, I don't mind. I am better, since my head is not hurting. Thank you for allowing me to take a hot bath. That was exactly what I needed," Kayla expresses to Mason.

The nurse helps Kayla from the wheelchair up to her bed, while Mason is on the phone ordering something to be brought to her room to eat. The nurse and Mason finish their tasks at the same time. The nurse turns and is walking out of the room, as Mason is turning his attention back to Kayla.

"I took the liberty of ordering you some food, but it will take some time to prepare. While we have this time together, I would like to talk about a few things with you, if you don't mind? I mean if you are up for a little conversation," Mason speaks to Kayla as he wants to befriend her, while holding something back, she suspects.

"That sounds like a splendid idea," Kayla replies back. Kayla is eager to get some information of her own from Mason. She also wants to see if the memories she received will take over on their own, or if she will have to try and find them to use them.

"Great, first let's start with, how do you know Alexis?"

"Who's Alexis," Kayla replies back without hesitation. She feels something has been put in her mind as an automatic response whenever anyone asks her about Alexis.

"You mean to tell me you do not know the person who asks me to take you into my group?" Mason demands of Kayla.

"I am not sure what you are trying to get at here, Mr. Carpenter, but we both know I was not given to you by anyone. I have been a part of this group for many years, and we've been looking for the Time Keeper. I do remember that the last mission I was sent on went bad, and I got hit hard. I was hit hard enough to put me in a deep sleep. I'm going to assume it was a coma, by the looks of this room and the nurse who was sitting in here when I woke up. She looked pretty startled when I woke up and asked to speak to you, by the way. I must have been out for some time, but I can assure you my mind is fine and intact. Now, you can stop with the mind games and test and ask what is really on your mind," Kayla snaps back without missing a beat. *Guess the memories know when they are needed after all,* she is surprised.

"Well, judging by your mood, you are a bit testy at this moment," replies Mason, as the food he ordered for Kayla is arriving. "Well, you are just in time, since she may be hungrier than I first anticipated," Mason is speaking to the orderly who has brought in the food. "Why don't you go ahead and eat, then get a bit of rest. I think once your body gets some solid food in it, and you are able to rest on your own, you will be more inclined for a civil conversation," Mason says as he is letting the person with her food in, while he exits the room.

Kayla is more than ready to accept the food he had ordered for her. She does not care what he ordered, because she is hungry and that is all that matters at this moment to her. Kayla takes the tray of food being offered to her and sets the tray down right on the bed in front of her, lifts the lid and smiles. She cannot believe Mason ordered her chicken and mashed potatoes. *Thank you Alexis,* she thinks to herself as she grabs a chicken leg and begins to eat. Kayla continues to eat until the tray is empty.

Kayla now has a full stomach, has taken a hot bath, and her head is not hurting. She just wants to lay back and try to rest on her own, which does not take her long, once her eyes close. She's able to sleep and start sorting through the memories she was given. Now she is able to tell the difference between the real and the fake memories. The real ones, or the truth, are for her, and the fake ones, those are for her protection. Kayla grows bored of going through those memories as soon as she starts. The importance of the memories does not escape Kayla, but she decides she wants to try something else. Kayla wants to try and reach out to Ian one more time.

Kayla stops thinking of the other memories given to her and pulls all her energy together to focus on one short message to send to Ian.

"Don't forget me Ian," is all she can come up with, with the amount of energy she can force from her body. She hopes the amount of energy she was able to pull together was enough, before she herself was out cold, back into a deep sleep.

Robert Starnes

Chapter 16

In the End

Ian was tossing and turning, fighting against an ache that was inside of him, pulling him between his dreams and someone else's memories. The harder he tries to resist, the more Ian finds it difficult telling the difference between them. Once Ian learned about the Time Keeper and the memories which the Time Keeper held, he was able to tell the difference between a dream and an actual memory, but whatever is causing this pulling between the two is mixing them up. He is now more determined to take back some control over his life. Ian starts by trying to take back some control over the powers of the Time Keeper, by simply forcing himself to dream instead of being forced to see someone else's memories.

After hours of fighting against the unknown force, Ian can no longer fight against whatever has been pulling against his mind. He gives up the control and lets it pull him into the dream, or memory, it wants him to see. Ian relaxes his mind to give full control over to the forces that be, and in doing so, images in his mind start to clear up. He is seeing clear visions of people and a room where they are being held. Once Ian's mind is fully relaxed and he has let the power take full control over his mind, he knows this is not a dream, but something else. *This is not a dream, or a memory from the Time Keeper. This is something I've never gone through before, from someone I've never met*, Ian thinks to himself in pure wonder.

Now that Ian has figured out that this is not his powers doing this, he becomes curious to find out more. Ian wants to understand whose mind he is in, and who is showing him these images. Has he been pulled into someone else's mind, or is someone in his mind showing him these visions? The one person he knew it was not showing him these images was Kayla. Kayla had come and said her goodbye. *Kayla is not coming back*, Ian thought. *I am going to take a look around and figure out what I'm dealing with here.*

In his dream state, Ian is standing in the middle of a white room. The room appears to be without any doors or windows, only four white walls, a white floor and a white ceiling. To him, it is as if he is standing inside a large white square box. As Ian's vision becomes clearer, the people he first saw vanish. There appears to be no source from which the light is coming from within the solid white room, but the room is a bright white room now. Ian is not in control of this vision, and he feels someone else is in the room with him, but they do not want to be seen, not yet. The presence of the other one in the room lets Ian know he won't wait long until they reveal themselves to him, so he will wait.

The emotions and feelings from the one in control grow inside Ian. Then a little girl and boy appeared on the other side of the room from him. They are not very clear for him to see and their voices are muffled for him to hear. The harder Ian tries to clear their image and voices, only makes them worse. The one in control is not ready to show them to Ian, but Ian can tell that they are important to him somehow. Then, during the blurred vision, the boy stops moving, but the girl does not stop moving. She's acting, or feeling, like she's done something wrong. "What is going on, why is she so scared? What's happening to the little boy?" Ian thought aloud. "Why am I being shown these children if I can't help them?"

The new vision that had appeared, of the small boy and girl, is now fading away. The one in control is ready to show Ian another vision. This time the vision came quicker, not any clearer, but much quicker. From what Ian can make out at first, there is a clock. This clock is inside a store or building, due to the vision being blurry and quick, it could be anywhere. The next thing Ian hears is the loud sound of a train whistle and the sounds of a moving train along the train tracks. Once the train sounds subside, in an instant, Ian beings flipping upside down, around and around, back and forth, as the room is rushing with water. Ian is not expecting water to fill the room, so he is caught off guard. To be honest, Ian was not expecting any of what was happening. The air is being pushed from Ian's lungs, but before panic can take over, Ian remembers he is in a dream. Even though Ian is in water, he could breathe. He feels being able to breathe in water is not what he is to take from this vision, but it is the water itself that is the actual point of the vision.

The water is gone, and Ian is standing alone in the middle of the bright white box again, and he is dry as bone. As if the one in control could anticipate Ian was about to ask a question, the bright white room turns to a bright red. It was the same color red each of the focus items were in the memories Ian was shown.

"I am not sure what you are wanting me to learn from these visions, but I connected this color red to my dreams, or the memories, already. So why should you show me red now?" Ian inquires aloud. Ian did not expect an answer back, but to his surprise the red room reveals something to Ian about the one in control, which he does not think was intentional.

Ian now understands that the one in control may foresee many things, but that does mean the knowledge they have is complete, or the changes in history have not caught up to them yet. These things that have been shown to Ian, so far, are things new to him, except the last one with the color red. *Is the one in control now, the same one that was in control of my other dreams? If they are, how could they not recall all the previous memories having the same color red or me having access to the Time Keeper?* Ian wonders to himself.

In a flash the red is gone; the room returns back to white, but this is a much brighter white this time. It's as if the comment Ian makes about the color red caught the one in control off guard. The room begins to dim, as the setting starting turning into a city. To Ian, the setting could have been any city, any city filled with tall buildings. Then Ian makes out a group of five people, who appear as part of the setting. Even though the group of five is blurry to him, just like the children were, Ian can tell he is one of the five he is seeing now. The little boy and girl are the blurry ones from his first vision from tonight's dreams, and Jax is there as well, but there is a taller blonde boy with them, which Ian does not know. Then the vision is gone, and the white room is back to normal.

Once the room is returned to its basic, bright white, box of a room, Ian can tell the time has come. Ian knows it is time to meet the one in control. Ian is not sure if he is ready for this introduction or not, but he also knows that it is not up to him. Without warning, the pressure in the room starts to build, and build up fast and hard, pressing against Ian's body. The pressure is building so fast, it causes pain to rush throughout Ian's body, head and mind. The room begins to flutter with different shades of colors and places at a rapid pace. Ian is in far too much pain to even try and focus on any one place or color, just to try to see if anything could give him an idea of who he is about to meet. The more he tried, the weaker he became, because everything went faster and faster, forcing him to abort trying to figure out anything about the colors or places. All at once it all came to an abrupt stop, the pressure building, the pain, and then Ian is suddenly standing on top of a skyscraper. Ian takes a few minutes to compose himself. He wants to be sure he has a clear mind when he finally meets the one in control.

"Ian, before you turn around, I want to tell you that I didn't mean to put you through the pain you just went through. I was not sure if I would even be able to reveal myself to you to begin with, much less know it would cause such pain to you," a voice speaks, from behind Ian, with a hint of sadness.

The voice speaking does not sound familiar to Ian, as he turns around, all he can think is, *who can this be?*

Ian is now face to face with the stranger, the one who has been in control of his dreams, and he still cannot place him. "Who are you?" Ian comes right out and asks the, now visible, stranger.

"My name does not matter at this moment, but for the purpose of this meeting, you may call me Junior," replies the one in control. "Please forgive my intrusion into your mind, but there are some things I need to tell you, or in a better way, show you. However, a comment you made while I was in the process of showing you those things, left me puzzled. Then I felt it. I felt the change. I felt what you meant when you said you had connected the color red to the memories you had been shown already. Although I did not get that feeling from you, but through a time ripple which is now catching up with my time. There is not much time left for me now. The things I was in the process of showing you do not matter now since history has been changed in such major ways. It seems that someone else has succeeded and made it to you before I could. Now, what has been done can't be undone. You already understand that you will gain access to memories stored in the Time Keeper once you turn eighteen, again, right? Well, the reason you don't remember being at school while you were seventeen for the first time is because of me. I knew I had little time to work with, so I had to move you forward a year. I needed you to be eighteen in order for me to force your powers to unlock the Time Keeper. I needed you to be able to access the Time Keeper in order for me to communicate with you in the beginning. That was the only way I was able to show you the memories stored in the Time Keeper. Of the four memories I did show you, you know two of them were from the past, one was of the present, and one is of, what you will say is the future. Remember when you woke up in the taxi and noticed the time difference and how day turned to night as you crossed over the Manhattan Bridge? Well, you were not leaving Central Park after looking for your parents like you thought. You were actually heading back from the last memory I had shown you. This may be a lot to take in and be a bit confusing, but time can be a little tricky and exists in multiple realms. I'm guessing that right now you think the life you are living is the only reality in time," states Junior.

"Okay, I have to admit that I'm lost. What do you mean the only reality or multiple realms? I know this is not reality, this is a dream, or memory, that you want me to view. Yes, I know that history has changed, but it was not done by me. It was done by someone else. We are not sure how, or why, but my best friend erased herself from history, and I'm the only one who can remember her," Ian replies.

"Your friend, what is her name?" Junior demands.

"What does her name matter? Like I said, I am the only one who can even remember she existed," Ian shoots back.

"Her name, please, just humor me. Remember, time is something of which I do not have much left," Junior pleads to Ian.

"Kayla. Her name is Kayla," Ian answers.

"Mom," whispers Junior.

"What did you say?" Ian cannot believe what Junior whispers.

"Nothing. I now understand why time has changed, or is about to. I wish I was able to get to you sooner. I'm sorry Ian. I am so sorry I could not save you both. I must go now, but I can tell you one thing for sure, you don't need to look for Kayla anymore. I can tell you one thing is for sure, and that is, she is gone," Junior tells Ian.

"How can you be so sure that she is gone?"

"I am sure Ian, because I'm fading from the future timeline. Kayla, you see, is my mother, so without her, there will be no me. Since I am fading that means she is gone," Junior replies as he vanishes.

"Kayla is your mother? Wait, don't go Junior. What are you talking about?" Ian is shouting.

Junior fades from Ian's time. His connection with Ian's mind fades along with him. Ian's mind returns back to his own dreams and his own body. Juniors' release of Ian's mind back to him is instant, and that's when he can feel that Junior is gone. Ian cannot stop the overwhelming sense of pain for his loss, not only the loss of his best friend Kayla, again, but now the knowledge of her son, the son she will never give birth to and be a mother to. Her son, who was trying to stop her from erasing herself from time, even though he didn't know it was her, was too late.

Ian suddenly rises up in his bed. In shock and shaken by what he just went through, his head is spinning with so many thoughts, *What is reality in real time and is there more than one, and WHEN does Kayla go back to next year to erase herself and how? How can she access the Time Keeper?* Ian let his mind run wild. Ian, being overwhelmed with everything that he learned, the things he knew and could process, and the things he could not, took so much energy from him, all he could do was fall back on his pillow, closes his eyes, and fall back to sleep. This time he hears nothing at all and sees nothing at all. He has no interruptions, until...

"Don't forget me Ian."

Ian's eyes shoot open. "Kayla," is his only word.

Epilogue: The Council

Junior is fading away from communicating with Ian while he sleeps. The Council is now aware of the change in history as well. They do not know what has changed, but they do know a very significant change has happened.

The Council begins reaching out to every special group leader. The Council has been waiting to see if any of them feel any changes in their kinds' history. They all reported back as to having no changes, meaning the change could only be a change in human history.

The Council narrows the event down to a human history. There is only one person they can turn to for help and her name is Alexis. The Council begins to reach out to Alexis through her family, but to their surprise, no one in her family has ever heard of her or of anyone named Alexis. The Council can tell that something is wrong.

Since they have been watching Ian and herself, so closely for many years they believe Alexis has to be somewhere in time.

The Council continues their search by going back and looking into their own records. They begin with birth and death records searching for Alexis, and while they can remember her, their records show no birth of her. Their own records show no existence of 'Kayla Alexis' of ever being born. That's the moment when the Council realizes the change in history is, in fact, Alexis going back and erasing herself.

With the Council having no way to travel back in time, they are going to call upon the help from some of the other beings, whom the Council has been watching over the years, which may be able to go back in time, so they can try and stop Alexis from erasing herself from history.

Ian's search for a way back in time, to save his best friend Kayla begins, and so does the Council's, but both for different reasons.

Only time will tell who will succeed.

Acknowledgements

I would like to thank my brother Pete for the amazing painting which is the very colorful part of the cover art you see on "Time Keeper". As you can see, that is his signature on the bottom right of the cover. I can't wait to see want you have in store for book two, "School Bound".

Next, I would like to thank my editor, Pat with Carpenter Editing Services, LLC. She has been a second mother to me for many years and with her editing skills, advice, and opinions on "Time Keeper", this work of art would not be what it is today. She worked so diligently day and night with spot on ideas, which I am grateful for. I am super excited for her as well, as she has prepared a syllabus this book, and will also do the same for the others in the series for Teachers. That is another reason we work so well together, we are both about teaching.

I could not leave out a thank you to the rest of my family for allowing me to use their names as the majority of my characters. I chose my family for character names, because my family members are all characters in their own way. They are in no way like their characters in this book, but they are all very special and unique people in their own right. "Jax" is one of my heroes and is also one of the reasons for this book series. My nephew Jaxon is an amazing special child, with two loving parents, my little brother John Dock and my sister-in-law Jessica. They also raised a lovely daughter, whose name is left out for a reason; she will be introduced in the next book along with my little sister Ashley's son. Thank you to Kayla and Alexis for joining book one.

Last, but not least, I would like to give a quick thank you to the many places that allowed me to sit and write in their establishments when I needed that creative energy. A few of those places are Skyhouse Main (in Houston, TX), The Carter (in Houston, TX), The Shoppe (in Houston, TX), Overtime Grill and Bar (off Lakeshore Pkwy in Birmingham, AL), Dunkin Donuts (off HWY 119 in Pelham, AL) and 700 Riverchase (in Hoover, AL). Without these places listed I would have been lost, because as someone with ASD, social settings are not easy for me, and I never felt out of place or any pressure at these creative energy spots. These places made me feel at home every time.

Robert Starnes

Continue along with Ian, as he continues to find a way to save his best friend, Kayla, in *School Bound*.

Saving History - Time Keeper

An Exciting and Adventurous way to view History

Book Two of the

Saving History Series

School

Bound

Robert Starnes

Robert Starnes

Prologue: Council's Choice

With the Council being unable to use Alexis to repair the change in history, since she is the one who caused the change in history by going back and erasing herself from it, their choices for help are limited. There are only a couple of other special groups they watch over that may be able to help them go back in time. The Council isn't in agreement on who they can turn to for help. They know no one can fully be trusted, when before they all could agree on Alexis for help.

Knowing the struggles they are faced with after months of debating among themselves, the Council reached a decision on who they would reach out to for help. They have agreed to seek help from three groups they have been watching for many years that have the most potential of being able to complete such a task that they will be asking them to do. Picking the groups to ask to help them go back in time to stop Alexis is just the first obstacle they are going to face. They still have a few more obstacles to overcome if they are going to succeed.

Unaware of Alexis' true intentions on why she went back in time and erased herself from history, or at least a version they are aware of that she does exist in, they can only make assumptions between themselves. The Council does not believe in assuming anything, only in facts, so this has them at a loss and confused. This is new for them, to not be in the know, or even in control.

The one thing they can agree on is going back to stop Alexis from erasing herself is their top priority at this moment, so they send out their request to the leaders of the three groups they have chosen for help. They do understand that each one will want something in return, even if they are unable to achieve their goal sending them back in time, but they have to try.

While their formal, yet urgent, request to the group leaders they chose have been sent out to attend a Special Council Meeting, they can only wait and see if they accept the invitation.

So their wait begins...

Chapter 1

Why Michael?

Ian has been awake for two hours before his mother knocked on his bedroom door. He knew today was coming quickly, and he has been anxious to go to school, so he could begin his search for Kayla. Ian knows she is still out there, somewhere in time, since it has only been a week since her last contact with him. Her last words to him where "Don't forget me, Ian," and he has no intention of doing so. He was up and ready to go to his new school with Jax.

"It's time to get up."

"Thanks, mom," Ian replies, knowing it will be some time before he is able to come back home to see his parents. Today, Jax is going to be taking him to his new school.

"What do you want for breakfast this morning?" his mother asks.

"How about my favorite, eggs over medium, toast, and today, make it a tall stack of buttermilk pancakes," Ian replies. Ian is not sure for how long it is going to take them to get to his new school, so he wants to make sure he eats enough this morning to last until, who knows when, they will stop to eat again.

Jax has told Ian very little about where the school is actually located. Ian was just told to pack for at least a full semester. Packing for long term only let Ian know he was going to be at school awhile, but not exactly how long it was going to take them to get there, not to mention how they were going to get there.

Surely, we will be flying to the school, Ian secretly hopes. *What if the school is not even in the United States? I don't even have a passport!*

Okay, calm down and relax, he tells himself. *If I needed a passport, I'm sure Jax would have told my mother and me beforehand.*

I better get a move on, Jax could be over at any moment and I still need to get ready, Ian begins to motivate himself.

Being the snappy dresser Ian is, and since today is a special day, he wants to make sure he looks his best when they arrive at his new school. *You can only make a first impression once,* Ian thinks to himself.

Before Ian's shower, he had already laid out a pair of dark jeans, a crimson long sleeve button down dress shirt, black leather dress belt, black vest and bowtie, all topped off with a pair of black socks and black tennis shoes. He wants to not only look good walking around today, but he also wants his feet to feel good.

After Ian finishes his shower and dries off, he brushes his teeth and combs his hair. Ian has shoulder length, naturally curly black hair. Being that his hair is naturally curly, Ian normally just lets it hang down, but since today will be spent traveling, he pulls it back with a rubber band. Pulling his hair back is the best way for it to stay out of his face for the long trip.

Ian takes his time getting dressed this morning, because he is a little scared to be leaving home. This will be the first time he has ever been away from home without his parents or his best friend Kayla, even though no one remembers her except him. Just as Ian is about to put on his ring, there is a knock on his bedroom door. Ian sets the ring down next to the Time Keeper on the dresser.

The Time Keeper is the watch that was created by Peter Hele, Ian's distant relative. Ian has recently found out the watch's history and how his family bloodline can access it. Not only can he access the Time Keeper, but the memories that have been stored in it by his past relatives, who had possession and control of it during their time period. His ancestors have had the ability to gain access to the Time Keeper where they could store any memory they wanted to store in it and access their own memories as well. Not many of his ancestors ever used the Time Keeper to go back into their memories to change the outcome for fear of the effects it could have in their current time. Really, only one of Ian's ancestors used it enough for the Council to take notice of the Time Keepers' existence, and that was Sebastian Helen. Of course, Sebastian never used it in a way to change history, except only to keep his friendship intact with Greyson Zimmerman. It works up until one night's fight causes Sebastian to lose the Time Keeper, not forever, but for a very long time.

Up until recently, it has always been believed that one could only access their own memories that they stored in the Time Keeper. That all changed when Ian lost a year of his life, after leaving his apartment to look for his parents, on his first seventeenth birthday, only to come home to his surprise eighteenth birthday party. Confusing as it was already, when Ian went to bed that night, he woke up back on his seventeenth birthday again, not being able to remember any of year he lost from turning seventeen to eighteen.

Now the ring, which Ian sets the Time Keeper next to on the dresser, is the birthday gift Kayla gives him on his eighteenth birthday, next year. That silver ring, when placed on Ian's hand while he is wearing the Time Keeper, wiped Kayla from history and sent him back to his seventeenth birthday. Kayla was able to contact Ian and explain some of why she did what she did. She also explained that now Ian has an extra year to go back to the school to learn more about what's to come, so he'll know more than he knew the first time. This is the time he lost between seventeen and eighteen.

He has been ready to get to school since Kayla last contacted him, in his dream, a week ago.

The knocking continues as Ian asks, "Who is it?"

"It's me, Michael," is the reply.

Michael? What in the world could he be doing here? Ian wonders in confusion. He turns to open his bedroom door, almost tripping over the bag he has already packed for school.

"What are you doing here?" Ian questions Michael.

Michael has been Ian's biggest bully throughout school. Ian had never done anything to him, but Michael had it out for him for as long as Ian can remember. *This must have something to do with the change in history. At least I hope it does,* Ian contemplates.

"Well, do you really think I'm going to let you leave for a new school and not come by and see you off?" Michael answers. "Besides, we never got to finish our talk about what happened to you the other day, remember, on your birthday?"

"Yes, I remember, but there really isn't much to talk about," Ian is holding back the truth from Michael, because he has no clue what he is talking about. "After you left and I went to talk to my parents, they surprised me with this whole 'new school' thing."

"All right then, if you say so, Ian. So, tell me about this private school where your parents are sending you," Michael says with excitement for Ian.

Ian knows very little about the school he is about to go to or even where it's located. He never asked Jax about it. Once time was thought to be healed, from the intentional history wipe, the question never came up.

"You know Math, English, History, the usual classes like any other school. Just new people," Ian tells him.

"Enough about me and the school, let's talk about you," Ian playfully suggests to Michael. "What are you going to do?"

"Well, for starters, I just may start getting to school on time, now that I won't have to wait for you to get ready in the mornings," Michael smirks at Ian.

"To be perfectly honest, Ian, I haven't really thought about it. I mean, it's going to take some getting used to, you not being here. I guess I will just have to hang out with my other friends more," Michael admits.

"Breakfast is ready," Ian's mother is yelling from the kitchen before Ian can make any remarks back to Michael.

"Do you want to stay for breakfast? We are having my favorite!" Ian asks Michael, trying to persuade him into believing he knows they are friends.

"I can't, sorry. My mom is taking me shopping for some reason," Michael tells Ian. "Will I see you on winter break?" Michael asks Ian with a sad look on his face.

"I'm not sure, but let's just say that when I do come back, you will be the first person I call. I promise," Ian says to Michael.

"Deal, now go eat your breakfast before it gets cold. I'm headed into the city with my mother for the day. Wish me luck," Michael orders Ian.

As they both say their goodbyes and give each other a farewell hug, Ian couldn't help but wonder what else has changed, now that Kayla is no longer in his past or in history for that matter. Now that Michael is his best friend, Ian misses Kayla even more.

As Ian takes a seat at the table to enjoy his breakfast, he hears the front door close behind Michael as he leaves.

Just as Ian is about to take a big bite of his pancakes, Jax comes rushing in the front door. "Ian, are you all right?"

"Yes, why does everyone keep asking me that?" Ian replies. "What's wrong?"

"I'm not sure, yet. There has been a change in time. Did you go back and change something?"

"No, I couldn't even if I wanted to, remember I'm only seventeen. I won't be able to access the Time Keeper until I'm eighteen," Ian answers, while running to his room to grab the watch. "Anyway, you can see for yourself the Time Keeper is right here, and so is the ring!" Ian yells while holding the watch out in front of him in one hand and the ring in the other for Jax to see. After seeing them, Jax is satisfied knowing Ian still had them and had not used them. Ian wraps the watch around his wrist and slips the ring over his right hand ring finger first knuckle.

How am I going to explain this to Michael that my new History teacher came bursting in my front door, just as he was leaving? Ian wonders to himself.

"What did you say to Michael when you passed him as you were coming in just now?" Ian asks Jax.

"I didn't pass anyone on my way in," Jax answers looking puzzled at Ian.

"That's not possible! He just walked out of the apartment when you burst in! You had to have passed him, if not in the hall, then in the stairwell. He has to live somewhere near here!"

"Are you sure, Ian? Who is Michael anyway?" Jax asks Ian sharply.

"Yes, I'm sure. He just left. For some reason, since Kayla is no longer part of my history, I think this guy Michael from school is now my best friend, except, I don't remember anything about us being friends," Ian explains to Jax. "It's a long story."

"What is all the commotion about? Jax, what's happening?" Ian's mother demands to know as she is flying out of the kitchen.

"Mom, is Michael in the kitchen with you? Did he come back inside?" Ian needs to know.

"No. It's just me in here. I haven't seen Michael this morning. Was he here?" she inquires.

"What do you mean you haven't seen him this morning? Didn't you let him in about twenty minutes ago?" Ian asks.

"What are you talking about, Ian? No one has been here that I know."

"Michael was just here, in my room. He said he came over to see me before I left for school. If you didn't let him in, then who did?"

"Why in the world would Michael, of all people, come over here to see you off to school? You two have never been friends," his mother replies back with a little concern in her voice.

This is the moment when Ian begins to think of a new conclusion.

Ian grabs Jax by the arm and pulls him over to the hall, towards his room. Jax gives him a look of surprise, but follows along with his guidance.

Once they are alone, and out of earshot of his mother, Ian decides to tell Jax what he believes to be happening. "You told me that time had healed and had caught up to our new reality, the one without Kayla, correct?" Ian asks Jax.

"Yes, I told you that yesterday, which is what the Council told me. Why do you ask?"

"I don't think that was the truth. I think time is just now catching up to our reality and healing, because that is the only explanation as to why you did not run into Michael just now as you were entering the apartment. Michael had just left here and closed the door, and then a few seconds later you came in, but you didn't see him at all. If you didn't see him, then where did he go? While we are on the subject, do you remember where you were just before you came through our door?" Ian questions Jax.

"Of course I remember where I was. I was coming over here. I was..."

"Was what?" Ian asks for Jax to continue.

"Well, I know I was headed here, because I had just received a call from the Council about another force felt by them. The only thing is that

I don't remember the trip here. I do remember reaching for my front door, to leave my apartment, then being here," Jax explains.

"And that doesn't sound or feel odd to you?"

"Not really. When I think about it, the memory of me coming here is in my mind, except it is more of a fast memory. It is like watching a movie, but in fast forward. It's hard to explain, but I do and don't remember coming over here. It is just when I think about it, it's in fast forward and I can't control it, so I can't stop it at any point, or even slow it down. Do you understand?"

"Well, kind of. It sounds a lot like what I went through with the memory wipe, except instead of your memories going in reverse, yours were going forward, fast forward," Ian reiterates to Jax.

"If what you are suggesting is true, and time is just now catching up and actually healing, then we may already be behind schedule," Jax relays to Ian.

Right then, Jax decides it is time for them to leave and head for the school. Jax hopes Ian's mother still knows about Ian going off to school.

"Well, we really should be hitting the road. We have a long trip ahead of us today. What do you say, Ian, are you ready to go?" Jax shoots Ian a look of, please trust me.

"Okay, let me grab my bag," replies Ian, as he runs back to his room to get his packed bag.

Now that Ian has everything and they are heading out of the apartment, they run into Michael, Ian's now best friend, as he was walking up to the door.

"Ian, where are you going? You weren't going to run off to school without telling me bye, were you?" Michael has a shocked look in his eyes as he questions Ian.

Feeling overwhelmed, Ian suddenly feels dizzy. Panic is starting to take over his mind, and that is when IT happened. Ian didn't know what was going on. One minute he's running out of the apartment with Jax, and the next minute everyone freezes, except for Ian.

What did I do this time? Ian wonders, in amazement, to himself.

"What did 'you' do?" replies a voice Ian has never heard before. "You mean 'what did I do,'" says the voice again. The voice sounds like it is coming from the stairwell.

About that time, a young girl comes walking out from the stairwell door. The young girl couldn't be more than ten years old. The girl is small, but has the biggest hazel green eyes and long curly blonde hair. She looks lost and anxious, her big hazel eyes looking everywhere around her, while biting her nails. She is trying to remain calm.

"What's your name?" Ian asks the little young blonde girl.

"Kenzie," replies the girl. "My name is Kenzie."

About the Author

Robert Starnes is the author of The Multifamily Housing Guide – Leasing 101, Garden Style Edition. It is the first in a series dedicated to the Multifamily Housing Industry professionals. He, himself, has dedicated almost two decades to the industry and wanted to make sure anyone that is looking to begin a career, his first career passion, have all the tools they need to succeed as he has.

After being diagnosed with Asperger's Syndrome, which it is now part of a broader category called ASD (Autism Spectrum Disorder), at the age of 43, things started to click with him. After being able to identify and manage the parts of ASD he had, he was able to hone in on his creative writing. At a young age he did not like to read, because he had difficulty with the words on the pages in front of him. He knew the words and understood them, but his brain would comprehend them faster than his voice would speak them. This would cause him to either leave out words, or cause him to read very slowly so he could have his eyes go back over the words again, two to three times, before his voice caught up with his brain. This embarrassment would stop him from reading for many years.

After being an adult for many years, learning to face his fears, he began to read John Grisham books. He loves the law and movies, so it was perfect for him to read the "The Last Juror" before watching the movie. After reading such a great novel then watching the movie, he quickly learned he enjoyed comparing the differences between the novels and the movies. That was all it took for him to begin to enjoy reading for the first time. For many years he would only read novels that were going to become movies, because that was what he enjoyed about reading. After many years, once he read another novel that became a movie, but they never completed the movie series. The novel was so good that he completed the book series, which in turn gave him a new enjoyment for reading without the novels becoming movies.

With this in Robert's mind, he has written his series for anyone that may be going through the same things he went through as a child, or adult, with reading, and is trying to find a way for them to connect with the world of reading. He believes that you can read and write a perfectly great action packed novel that does not have to be 800 pages thick to be accomplished. He believes giving someone the opportunity and a way to enter the world of reading, then that's the accomplishment. No one should be afraid to read or write in their own style for others to be able to want to read. His mind does not work the same as a traditional writer's does and retains things much more than another person's may, so you will not find very much repeating, or recapping, in his series. You will find action, adventure, and history from the very first chapter to the very end.

To Robert, everyone is different and unique, and should be celebrated every day for being just who they are. He finds that when life may get you down, you can always get away in your own imagination with the help of a good book.

Robert Starnes

Books by Robert Starnes

Saving History Series:

Time Keeper – Starnes Books LLC (2018)
School Bound – Starnes Books LLC (2019)

The Multifamily Housing Guide Series

Leasing 101: Garden Style – Starnes Books, LLC (2018)

The Multifamily Housing Guide – Leasing 101 Garden Style Edition – Lulu's publishing (2016 retired print)

Robert Starnes

CPSIA information can be obtained
at www.ICGtesting.com
Printed in the USA
FFHW020051210719
53758371-59459FF